"How Much Longer Does This Party Go On?"

"The band is almost finished," Emma said, tearing her gaze away to glance at her watch. "This is the last set."

"Then we should make the most of it, shouldn't we?" he asked, pulling her over to the dance floor.

As Simon and Emma stepped onto the platform the band launched into the sweet strains of "Moonlight Serenade," the final number, and a strange feeling of unreality settled over Emma as she went into Simon's arms. This was what she had been waiting for, this was the only thing she wanted, and she couldn't believe it was happening.

They moved together a little stiffly at first, but then the music took over and, abandoning the pretence that they were any ordinary couple, they pulled each other into a tighter embrace, letting their bodies communicate in a language that words could not match.

Dear Reader,

Welcome to Silhouette! Our goal is to give you hours of unbeatable reading pleasure, and we hope you'll enjoy each month's six new Silhouette Desires. These sensual, provocative love stories are both believable and compelling—sometimes they're poignant, sometimes humorous, but always enjoyable.

Indulge yourself. Experience all the passion and excitement of falling in love along with our heroine as she meets the irresistible man of her dreams and together they overcome all obstacles in the path to a happy ending.

If this is your first Desire, I hope it'll be the first of many. If you're already a Silhouette Desire reader, thanks for your support! Look for some of your favorite authors in the coming months: Stephanie James, Diana Palmer, Dixie Browning, Ann Major and Doreen Owens Malek, to name just a few.

Happy reading!

Isabel Swift
Senior Editor

LAUREL EVANS
Moonlight Serenade

Silhouette Desire

Published by Silhouette Books New York

America's Publisher of Contemporary Romance

SILHOUETTE BOOKS
300 E. 42nd St., New York, N.Y. 10017

Copyright © 1985 by Laurel Evans

ISBN: 0-373-05248-0

First Silhouette Books printing December 1985
Second printing January 1986

America's Publisher of Contemporary Romance

Printed in the U.S.A.

LAUREL EVANS

began writing romances when she was working for a literary agent in New York. She lives in Louisville, Kentucky, and is currently working for the local newspaper.

One

It's 8:03 P.M. and in case you haven't noticed, folks, it's cold and rainy out there tonight. But spring is on the way, I have it on the very best authority, and if you keep your mackintosh oiled, next month this will be just a bad memory. You are supposed to oil a mackintosh, aren't you? Anyway, hope you're inside tonight. This is Emma of WLIT, Litchfield, *your* radio station." Emma carefully lifted one restraining finger off the record and let the sounds of the Glenn Miller Orchestra playing "String of Pearls" fill the tiny studio. She closed her eyes and listened to the first familiar bars that somehow still had the power to cause a tiny kernel of excitement to grow in the pit of her stomach, even after three years of playing it during her jazz program. It was perfect on a night like tonight, and Emma fondly believed it would warm people up just to hear it, the way it did her.

Always forcing herself to be practical, however, she leaned forward and flipped the microphone switch to Off, before lifting the foil cover from the bowl of soup Stu had brought up for her dinner. It was a savory fish chowder tonight, and she inhaled gratefully and took a large spoonful before delving into her bag for the corn muffin of her own making that was enclosed in plastic wrap. It was a light supper, but being a disc jockey was a fairly sedentary life and Emma certainly didn't think she needed anything more substantial.

She had just bitten into the muffin when the light flashed to signify an incoming call, and she swallowed hastily, choking on the crumbs and grabbing for a glass of water to keep herself from strangling. Requests were always welcome and she had absolutely no right to curse the caller who had interrupted her dinner, but by now Emma knew what Litchfield liked, and Litchfield knew what Emma had, and requests rarely came in during her jazz program. Clearing her throat one final time, she managed to croak "Hello?" into the mouthpiece of the telephone and then resumed coughing.

"I'd like to hear 'Kill' by Debby and the Deadbeats," a shrill young voice was saying over the sound of Emma's wheezes.

"This is a jazz program," she answered, recovering her naturally husky voice at last. "That's all we play on Thursday night. Isn't there something jazzy you'd like to hear? It doesn't have to be swing."

"I don't know any jazz," the voice answered shyly, after a moment of silence. It sounded as though it were ten or eleven years old, but she had no idea what its gender was.

"Well, listen. You might learn something," Emma cajoled. "And if you call tomorrow, somebody will play

'Kill' for you.'' She never knew whether the voice liked that idea or not, because the line simply went dead. Apparently most of the public didn't believe there was a real person sitting behind the microphone or that d.j.'s were deserving of simple courtesies such as "goodbye" or "thank you." This kid was no exception.

She sighed and set up her next selection, manually turned down the volume of "String of Pearls" for a fade out and smoothly cued the next record. It wasn't all that difficult to do, but by the time she was finished, her soup was on the chilly side. She spooned it up anyway and then turned back to give her full attention to the music, her own mellow voice blending in nicely with the dying wail of the tenor sax as she turned down the volume.

"That was Stanley Turrentine and 'I Haven't Got Anything Better to Do,' and I haven't got anything better to do than to read the latest forecast, which is for another day of rain, temps in the high forties to low fifties, and then, praise be, a dry and beautiful weekend, highs in the sixties and a lot of sunshine. Coming up in the next few hours we've got some Nat King Cole, some George Benson, some John Coltrane, and just to shake everybody up a little we'll start out with the master himself, Duke Ellington and 'Take the A Train.' Ever taken the A train, by the way? What an anticlimax. This is your radio station, Litchfield. Let me know what you want to hear."

She sat back in her swivel chair, rested her gaze on the rain that was spattering against the window with increasing force and wished in vain for a cup of coffee. Her office coffee maker had expired two weeks before, and she was trying to wait until she could find one on sale before buying a new one. As president and owner of WLIT, one of the founding mothers, as she put it, she wasn't sure she'd made the right decision. Everybody practically inhaled coffee on the job, and she seriously doubted she could sit through one more cold, damp evening without a steaming mug of something to clutch in her hands when they weren't busy. She made a mental note to go out and fork over whatever was necessary first thing in the morning, so that her young staff would have a slightly easier weekend. Emma herself rarely worked on the weekends, but she appreciated how difficult it was to do anything inside when spring was well on the way in the beautiful hills of Northwestern Connecticut.

For the next two hours she could easily have believed that she was talking to absolutely no one but herself. There were nights like that, sometimes, and she was used to putting herself almost on automatic pilot, calmly going through the pile of records she had selected earlier in the day, her own mindless patter filling the silences effortlessly. She hadn't thought she could ever get used to that part, talking to a whole horde of people she did not know and would never see. Actually, she realized bleakly, she was probably only talking to half a dozen people at most. And it had been surprisingly easy to just talk, to empty her mind of anything in particular and comment lightly on the music and the bits of trivia she knew about each number, or on current events, although she had to try to be nonpartisan most of the time.

The only issues she made no attempt to remain neutral on were those directly concerning Litchfield itself. It had been her home for seven years now and she took a fierce pride in it; she was determined that it stay just as safe and perfect as it had been when she had first moved up from New York City. It was a refuge, and she couldn't understand why anybody would ever want to change it. She was just musing on that when the telephone light lit up for the second time that evening, and this time she reached for it eagerly, tired of her own thoughts.

"Would you play 'I'm Getting Sentimental Over You'?" It was a baritone voice, and Emma tried to figure out if he was one of her regular callers. She didn't think he was.

"Which band?" she asked, just to make him say something else. She, too, happened to like that song, but she only had one arrangement of it, so the question was academic.

"Whatever you say."

"Tommy Dorsey be okay?" she suggested, leaning back to the shelf behind her and laying a practiced hand on the record. She knew the layout of those shelves better than she knew just about anything else in the world.

"That's fine." He didn't say goodbye or thank you, but Emma knew he was still there and she wondered if he was going to say something obscene. That happened pretty often, but usually only when the call was on the air, and for this program she had discovered people called more readily if their calls weren't broadcast. She preferred to think that anybody who liked her kind of music would not make an obscene call, but she wasn't quite that naive.

"You still there?" she finally asked, curiosity getting the better of her.

"How much longer does your show last?" he asked in response.

"Why?"

"Because I'm enjoying it," he said, amusement coloring his voice. Up until then his voice hadn't had much expression, as though he, too, were a little wary.

She relented. "About another hour."

"Do you look the way you sound?"

Emma sighed in disgust. "I knew it, you're just another pervert. Someday I'm going to make one of you people explain why you get such a kick out of that, but I've got better things to do tonight. Goodbye." She broke the connection abruptly and turned back to put the record she was holding on the available turntable, realizing too late that it was his request. "Oh, well," she sighed to herself. "May as well give a little pleasure to some lonely pervert. At least he has good taste."

When the light on the telephone lit up as soon as the song was over, she seriously debated not answering it, but that didn't seem quite ethical somehow. And there was always a chance, though a slim one, that it wasn't him. Cautiously, she picked up the receiver.

"Thank you for the song. And just for your information, I'm not a pervert. I was trying to tell you that you have a beautiful voice, but apparently I wasn't doing it very well."

Emma was completely disarmed. "Well, thank you," she said grudgingly.

"Do you?"

"Do I what?" she asked, just to be annoying. She knew exactly what he meant.

"Do you look the way you sound?" he repeated, undaunted.

Emma thought about it for a minute. "No," she said bluntly. She believed it was the truth. She had been told often enough now that her voice was sultry, and that word conjured in her own mind someone lean and dark and elegant. She found herself, on the other hand, to be absolutely ordinary. A little on the unfortunate side of ordinary, on a bad day. She was thirty years old, five feet seven inches tall, and not slender. Her friends told her that her figure was lush, but she herself felt that her hips were too round, that her ripe breasts were too full, and that there was altogether too much of her beautiful, pale flesh. She had brown, wavy hair that fell in graceful curls to her shoulders, long green eyes that turned almost emerald when she cried, which hadn't been in years, and a wide, expressive mouth that had a very faint line or two around it, although it was impossible to tell at a glance if they were laugh lines or pain lines. She looked fertile, not, to her own mind, sexy. She had played Mother Earth in a school play in the fifth grade, and she sometimes felt that that particular role had branded her for life.

"But you don't know how you sound to me." His voice was amused, as though this were some marvelous new game.

"I know exactly how I sound." She hesitated. "Would you like to request anything else? I can't tie up this line any longer." She had no idea why she had consented to talk to him this long. It was certainly against everything she had been taught, and every rule for her own employees, not to mention her better judgment.

"How about a cup of coffee?"

"I'm afraid I don't know that—" she began and broke off when he started laughing. "Oh. You mean a cup of coffee with you." For Pete's sake, what kind of an idiot are you, she asked herself furiously.

"That's what I had in mind, but if you'd like to play it as well, that would be fine." He still sounded as though he were laughing.

"I can't. I'm not finished here." Why on earth did she give him an excuse? Why didn't she just say no? Why didn't she tell him she was married or something?

"I know you're not. Let me bring it to you. I'd love to see that record collection."

"No!" she answered, sitting up a little straighter and shocked at the very idea.

"Oh, that's right. I might do something perverted, mightn't I? Well, why don't you meet me somewhere safe when you're through?"

"No, I don't think so, thanks, I—" she began, caution finally asserting itself.

"Oh, c'mon. Have pity. I'm here on a business trip and I don't have anybody to talk to." His voice sounded sweet and coaxing, and Emma found herself warming to him in spite of herself. Apparently he could sense by her silence that he was making some headway, because he began to press her even further. "My name's Simon Eliot and I'm staying at the Lyons Inn. Just come by for twenty minutes. We can have coffee in the lounge here. I'll meet you downstairs in about an hour. You get off at eleven, right? I'll be waiting in the lobby." He stopped, but he didn't hang up, and Emma realized he was not as certain she would be there as he apparently wanted to be.

"I don't know," she said, still slightly appalled that she was even considering it.

"I'm going to be waiting for you anyway, so come if you can. And Emma?"

"Yes?"

"You might consider putting on another record. You've been feeding everybody a lot of static for a good two minutes now."

Emma muttered a curse and hung up, hastily grabbing the next record in the stack and letting it start. She took another moment or two to get herself organized and to sort out the rest of her program, and then leaned back in her chair and contemplated what had just happened.

One thing was certain, and that was that Emma Beckett did not go out with strange men. Why had she even talked to him, let him think she might meet him? Boredom? On the other hand, this wasn't actually "going out." What could happen during a twenty-minute cup of coffee in the lounge at the Lyons Inn? It seemed that there was something a little unsavory about his being on a business trip, but the only reason she could think of was that he might have a wife somewhere who wouldn't approve of his drinking coffee with strange women. Well, if there was anything wrong with him, she would simply leave. She caught herself. What was wrong with her tonight? Even if there wasn't a thing in the world wrong with him, after twenty minutes, she would leave anyway.

After her divorce from Ralph Stenfield seven years before, Emma had found she had little use for the male sex in any particular way. She no longer felt terribly bruised by the experience of marriage, simply older and much wiser. She had fallen in love with Ralph when she was nineteen years old, completely and selflessly in love, finding in the young and ambitious law student an acceptable purpose in a life she hadn't otherwise figured out what to do with.

Emma was the youngest of three children, and the per-capita income in her family was a figure she still found dreadfully intimidating. Her oldest sister, Joan, was a well-established brain surgeon by the time Emma herself was finishing high school; and her brother, Philip, the middle child, had finished college in three years and begun his own business. Emma always had trouble describing precisely what Philip did because he had his various fingers in so many different pies, and she generally ended up telling people he was "a very successful businessman." Her father, Vinny, had retired early from the national news magazine where he was managing editor and begun writing novels, apparently never bothering to wonder whether or not he would be able to publish them. He was right not to worry. And Emma's preschool memories usually involved playing quietly in the cluttered office from which her mother ran one of the most prestigious art galleries in Soho.

When Ralph Stenfield came along and invited her to drop out of college and pay his rent while he was in law school, she had been only too happy to accept. She had been quiet and shy at the age of nineteen, full bodied and voluptuous in the Twiggy era, and the fact that Ralph had a use for her was flattering. And she had also prided herself on the fact that Ralph fit into her family so well. He, too, was dynamic and ambitious and it wasn't until they had been divorced for two years that Emma figured out that no one in her family had been able to stand him.

While Ralph spent the next four years struggling through school in New York, Emma worked for a local radio station, first as a gofer and then gradually moving up through the ranks and being given more and more responsibility. She had never taken any speech classes, and never even considered trying to become a disc jockey, but her work, her lovely speaking voice, her charm and her smart efficiency were noticed by everybody, especially by the program manager. He had taken her under his wing, encouraging her to explore her love for jazz until she became an expert on the big bands and urging her to make a future for herself in radio. But Emma had known that her own plans for the future had to wait until Ralph had established himself. Her turn would come, and while she loved her job, she was looking forward to going back to college. Ralph, however, found upon graduation that having a wife was more of an encumbrance than a helpmate and coolly asked for a divorce.

Emma had given it to him. She knew that some people sued for financial compensation in cases like that, but the last thing she wanted from Ralph was his money. Her principal reaction was that she could not bear to burden him with her presence since he no longer wanted it or needed it, and she protected herself by withdrawing into her shyness and divorcing him without any fuss. She felt bruised by the experience, humiliated and depressed, but what was worse was the blinding panic she felt when she realized she was financially on her own. She didn't want money from her family, but for the first time she sincerely wished she had inherited the ability to make it.

The support her family gave her was in the long run, however, better than money. They gave her emotional support; reminded her that she had, in fact, been earning her own living for a long time now; and took turns taking her away for weekends, the theory being that it wouldn't hurt to get her out of New York City now and then.

It was during one Memorial Day weekend with her sister that Emma discovered Litchfield. They had booked a room at the Lyons Inn and as soon as they drove past the wide green that stretched through the center of the little town, Emma felt something in herself unfold, spread out, calm down. When she returned to her job in New York, the program manager, her mentor and friend, decided providentially that it was high time he left the city as well.

Emma sniffed a little in fond remembrance as she gazed out at the damp, glistening streets. How could she ever repay Leo for having faith in her, for convincing her that he wanted her for her talent alone, for taking her with him when he bought WLIT and for allowing them both to get out of New York? Emma had been delighted to go. She put everything she had into the station, working at all aspects of the job until she was exhausted, and it had paid off. She had been surprised to wake up one day and realize that she no longer missed Ralph, no longer needed or wanted him. She was doing just fine all by herself. The once struggling station was flourishing, and when Leo had had a heart attack and moved to Florida three years before, she had been able to work out an easy payment schedule and buy it from him. As of two months ago, it was officially hers.

With the first flush of prosperity had returned, in part, some of Emma's self-esteem. It didn't take a genius to realize that she was just as capable of supporting herself as Ralph was, but with her badly shaken self-confidence, it had taken her a good five years. Her family's loving kindness was no substitute for proving to herself that she could manage on her own, and she felt enormously better about herself now. The experience had left her a little touchy about the life she had made for herself, by herself, in Litchfield, however, and determined to guard and protect it. She was wary about making new friends and tended to seek out only people who would not make inroads into her precarious independence the way, say, a lover might.

The next hour passed all too quickly for Emma's peace of mind. She put on "Moonlight Serenade" as her final selection, sitting back in her chair and closing her eyes as the music washed over her. She had hoped it would make her feel relaxed, but instead it made her wish she was on a dance floor, wearing a long, sparkly chiffon dress and swaying easily in the circle formed by a pair of strong arms.

She could see it all—the dress would be a soft, pale green, layered, with a close-fitting bodice, very old-fashioned. The anonymous pair of arms would be encased in the black sleeves of a tuxedo, with white cuffs peeking out at the end, the hands strong and large and well made. Unfortunately she could not see above the crisp white tucks of his shirtfront, and after one more graceful little turn to the music she let the picture fade. She had already said good-night to Litchfield, and all she had to do when the record stopped was turn off her equipment and put the studio to bed. She did a more thorough job of straightening up than usual, but she was finished all too soon and the moment of truth, as she thought of it, was upon her.

She was beginning to feel like a character in a soap opera. Was Emma Beckett going to risk disrupting her peaceful existence by having coffee with a strange man? A strange *business*man?

And what would Stu and Tony say? Tony, of course, had no right to say anything. Tony was a forest ranger at the Mount Tom State Park and Emma's companion for beer, pizza and an occasional movie, occasional simply because the one theater in town changed films only occasionally. Although he wouldn't like it, he had no right at all to object to her meeting other men, strange or otherwise. And Stu, her best friend, the waitress at the Towne Restaurant, the person responsible for Emma's daily bowl of soup, would be only too pleased. Stu thought it was just fine for her own life to lack romance. She had had a wonderful marriage for three years, until her young husband had been killed in a practice air force maneuver, leaving Stu with a broken heart and a daughter who was now ten years old. Stu found it impossible to accept that Emma was satisfied with her rather solitary existence and, as a personal and entirely unsolicited favor, would give a detailed report on any interesting, unfamiliar faces in the restaurant.

Of course, Emma reflected, she wouldn't have to mention it at all. That would save Tony's feelings, however irrational they might be, and save Stu from getting her hopes up. Emma could go ahead and do something uncharacteristic and probably a little unwise, and it could be her little secret. Other women did things like this all the time, she told herself. He had a nice voice, he liked good jazz, and it might be fun to meet someone new, even a businessman just passing through.

Her courage thus bolstered, she pulled on her trench coat, gathered her things, and went out into the quiet, deserted town. When she had first moved up from New York it had taken her a while to stop being nervous about walking through the town alone after eleven o'clock at night. There were occasional incidents, of course, as there were everywhere else, but there was very little violence and she soon learned to go about her business. The only precaution she took was to drive her car to work, instead of walking, when she knew she would be leaving late.

The rain had stopped temporarily but the air was still heavy and damp, and there was a light breeze that smelled like wet soil, an unmistakable smell of spring. She crossed the street to her little red Toyota and drove down past the green to the Lyons Inn, a huge, stately old white building that Emma rarely had any occasion to enter these days. She had had Thanksgiving dinner there with her family one year when she had broken her arm and couldn't prepare the family dinner according to their usual custom. Of course no one had wanted to forgo the trip to Connecticut, and convincing Emma to come back to New York was unthought of. She was musing on the memories of the last dinner as she looked for a parking spot, and she entered the building with a small smile on her face.

The downstairs lobby was about as deserted as the street had been in the center of town. The only visible sign of life was a bored-looking desk clerk who was slumped tiredly on a stool behind the reception desk. Emma stood for a moment and looked around, uncertain about what she should do next. He had probably expected her to show up five minutes after her program ended, and she had dawdled a bit. On the other hand, if he thought she would come up to his room to find him, he was wrong. Perhaps he had simply gotten tired of waiting and decided she wasn't coming after all. She felt a surprising stab of disappointment at that thought, and approached the desk clerk in the vain hope that there might be a message for her.

"I'm looking for a Mr. Simon Eliot," she said to the young man, who barely looked up at her, merely pointing his finger toward the corner instead of answering her verbally. Emma followed the direction of his finger and saw a rather secluded area with a fireplace, two large easy chairs and a sofa. Now that she was looking more closely, she noticed two legs extending from one of the chairs, although from this angle she could not see much above the ankles.

She approached cautiously, clearing her throat softly to give him some advance warning, but he still gave no indication that he was aware of her presence. She finally had to cross all the way around the chair before she was rewarded with a good view of the complete Simon Eliot.

He was slouching in the chair but Emma could still tell that he was tall, at least six feet. The body beneath the rumpled business suit appeared to be fairly well made, not too slender but not at all fat. No, she could see through the opened jacket that he was not at all fat. He had black, tousled hair that needed a trim, at least in the back; rather pale skin beneath a slight growth of beard; and heavy, long eyelashes that made him look adorably vulnerable as they rested on his upper cheek.

Adorable was actually the word that came to mind, but as Emma looked longer she was not sure it was appropriate. His mouth was slightly open, his face was turned to snuggle against the wing of the chair, and as she stood admiring him he gave a soft, peaceful snore. Mr. Simon Eliot was sleeping like a baby.

Two

Emma stared at him for another moment, her earlier feeling of disappointment returning to her. She wouldn't have minded having coffee with him. She wondered if she should leave a message with the desk clerk, who didn't look too cooperative, or just leave. Maybe she could pin a note to Mr. Eliot himself the way her first-grade teacher used to do to her pupils, a simple but effective way of communicating. She sighed and murmured, "Oh, well," under her breath before turning away, and then paused as his eyes began to open. And then she simply had to turn back and take another look at his eyes. "Baby blues," she found herself thinking. They were sky blue, innocent blue, and he was opening them slowly as if he knew just what the sight of them unveiled too quickly could do to a person like herself.

Still nestling against the back of the chair, he turned his head slightly to gaze back at her. But he made no other movement, and she thought he probably was not completely awake yet. Finally, however, he spoke. "Hi." He had a slight southern accent, she realized, and his voice was still deep and husky from sleep.

"Hi," she answered, smiling at him unconsciously. "I'm sorry I woke you up. Are you Simon Eliot?"

"Yes. I didn't think you were coming." He still looked disheveled and confused, and Emma had a sudden, horrid thought that he might be mistaking her for someone else, some other assignation, perhaps?

"I'm Emma Beckett," she said to clarify the situation immediately, holding her hand out to shake his.

"I know." He smiled and stood up in one movement, and the combination caused her heart to start pounding in a heavy, unfamiliar thud. He certainly was tall, and his quick, full smile gave his face the character that had been smoothed out of it in sleep. Now that he was fully awake he looked no longer innocent and adorable, and Emma found herself shaking hands with him a little numbly. "I'd know that voice anywhere."

He didn't let go of her hand immediately and she felt the beginning of that old, instinctive fear that set in whenever her safety, the sanctity of her refuge, was threatened. Part of her knew that she was being ridiculous, but she wanted out of this immediately. "Listen," she began, licking her lips nervously, "you must be awfully tired, and it's a lot later than I thought it would be, and I have a million things to do tomorrow, so why don't we just say good-night? It was nice to meet you but I really should be getting home now...." She trailed off uncertainly as his grip on her hand tightened, and she was suddenly afraid he wasn't going to let her go.

"You can't just leave. A deal is a deal," he said. "And since you woke me up, the least you can do is let me buy you a drink." His grip had moved to her elbow during the above speech and Emma found herself being gently steered toward a dimly lit doorway, from which she could hear the subdued noises of people talking softly. She also found herself, to her dismay, very much aware of the weight of his hand through her raincoat, and she was confused about whether he was being forward or whether it was acceptable for a strange man to hold her arm and walk her into a bar.

She certainly had no intention of having a drink, but she supposed she might as well have a cup of tea. He was right—a deal was a deal. The bar, once they entered, was dark and quiet, with candles in frosted glasses on each table that gave a much more intimate atmosphere than she would have wished. She had originally envisioned the brightly lit innocence of a coffee shop, but now that she was here she found the subdued hush strangely relaxing.

She settled herself in one of the deep, comfortable chairs, leaned back, and took stock of the situation. Simon Eliot was resting his head on one hand and looking at her with a faint little smile in one corner of his mouth, and although she was aware of a not unpleasant tension in the pit of her stomach, her predominant feeling was a desire to stretch and preen in the light of his gaze. There seemed to be something about her that he liked and she didn't think it was just her voice. Emma's friends all liked the way she looked, and Tony had made his attraction to her evident all along, but there was something about this stranger's obvious admiration that she found stimulating and exciting.

"Um, what kind of business are you in?" she asked when she decided they had been sitting in silence long enough.

"I'm a television producer. But business is a dull subject. How about you? Why are you here?"

Emma felt herself blushing and was glad the lighting was dim. "I don't know," she began. "I don't do things like this. I mean, I know in New York disc jockeys go out with people who call in during contests, but I don't think that's a very good idea. I guess I was...bored." She looked up at him, candor making her wide green eyes even wider, and was surprised to see that he looked amused.

"I'm sorry," he said, touching her wrist lightly where it lay on the table. "I should have stopped you, but I wanted to hear what you had to say. I meant, why are you living in Litchfield?"

"There's nothing wrong with Litchfield," she began, defensive and thoroughly embarrassed by her mistake. "It's a beautiful little town. It's perfect. I never want to live anywhere else!"

"That's quite a recommendation," he said rather dryly.

She disregarded him and continued. This was, after all, one of her pet subjects. "You can get a wonderful feel for history here. Did you know that many of the houses have been standing since the Revolution, and are still lived in and loved, sometimes by the original families? They've all been preserved, and not for tourists. Tourists can only see inside them one day a year."

"Yes, I know. And I agree it is a pretty little place. But it's also a static little place. Don't you feel stifled sometimes?" He was still leaning his head on his hand in a relaxed pose, but he was no longer sleepy and smiling, and Emma found the full force of his blue gaze disconcerting.

"Stifled by what?" she asked.

"You tell me. You said yourself you were bored."

"Maybe that has nothing to do with Litchfield," she mumbled, not at all pleased with the shape their conversation was taking. She was relieved when the waiter arrived for their drink orders. "I'll have tea," she said, hoping that small display of prudery on her part would keep the dialogue from becoming any more intimate.

Simon bested her there as well. "Skim milk," he ordered, and then flashed her a grin that looked disarmingly boyish for just a moment. "Doctor's orders."

"You have an ulcer?"

"Not yet, but she tells me I'm due for one if I don't slow down and start drinking my milk."

"And what makes you go so fast in the first place?"

He shrugged. "New York is a fast-moving town. I have to keep up. But I wouldn't live anywhere else."

"And what are you doing in Litchfield?"

He straightened up, looking decidedly uncomfortable while the waiter placed their drinks in front of them. "I guess if I don't confess now you'll never forgive me," he said, draining his milk under her suddenly watchful gaze as though to give himself a little false courage. "I, uh, I play squash with your brother two or three times a week," he said, making an attempt to sound conversational.

"So?" she prodded warily.

Simon sighed. "So I'm producing a documentary on Willis Edmonds and your brother suggested I talk to you."

Emma was still a bit puzzled. Willis Edmonds was one of the last truly great saxophone players from the big band era and it was true that she knew quite a bit about him, but she didn't consider herself an authority by any means. "What do you want to know about him?"

"I want to know if you'll introduce him at a testimonial dinner in New York this summer," he said quickly, ducking behind his milk glass to ward off the blows he apparently thought were forthcoming.

Emma stared at her teacup with a deceptively calm expression on her face as several unpleasant impressions came crowding in on her. One of them was that her brother had found a backhanded way to prod her out of her comfortable little nest, and that hurt her feelings. She always secretly suspected that her family thought she ought to come back to New York and make a go of it there, that you hadn't really succeeded until you'd succeeded in the city. Another was that while she had thought Simon was simply overwhelmed by the sexy sound of her voice, to the point that he hadn't been able to resist calling her, she had actually been auditioning without knowing it. He wasn't attracted to her. He wanted to hire her. And since she was undoubtedly attracted to him, she began to feel a little silly.

"No," she said, looking up to meet his watchful gaze.

"No?" he repeated questioningly.

"No. N. O. I will not introduce your speaker," she said, and then slipped her arms back into her raincoat and prepared to leave.

Simon watched her in amazement for a couple of seconds before he went into action. "Okay, okay, okay," he said, grabbing her arm as she started to rise and forcing her to fall back into her chair somewhat gracelessly. Emma's rage came slightly closer to the boiling point. "I'm sorry," he said. "Let's just forget I asked, all right?"

He kept his hold on her arm and rather than get into a tug-of-war which she suspected she would lose, Emma remained in her chair and waited for him to try to extricate himself from the situation.

"We did a little better when we talked about Litchfield, didn't we? I'm directly descended from a founding father, you know." he said with a little smile. "Ever heard of Increase Eliot?"

"Who?" she asked, considering letting herself be charmed.

"You must not know your history."

"I never finished college," Emma confessed quickly, without quite knowing why. She wasn't really ashamed, but it wasn't a fact that she liked to volunteer to a casual acquaintance.

"I was teasing you," he said, touching her wrist again lightly with one finger and smiling, looking earnest and almost shy, as though he were afraid her feelings might be hurt. "Old Increase is a smirch on the family name. He went off to join the Revolution and had his horse stolen the first day out, when he was about twenty miles out of town. He came walking back into town, all his belongings still on his back, and said that he couldn't fight now, because he had no horse. Of course, people in town offered him their horses, some even for free, but Increase allowed as to how it was God's will that he not fight, and refused. A few months later he vanished, and ended up claiming to be one of the primary settlers of parts of Kentucky and Virginia, but it's hard to verify a claim like that. Anyway, everybody always suspected that he just took his pack off his horse and set him free."

"Poor man," Emma said, laughing in spite of herself. "He was just a coward. There's nothing wrong with not wanting to fight."

"Of course there's nothing wrong with it. He just didn't have the guts to admit it." Simon leaned back in his chair with a satisfied smirk on his face. "My father's still trying to pay back his debt to his country."

"How?"

"He's career army."

"And what about you?" she asked, calculating quickly. He looked to be about the right age to have been drafted during the Vietnam war.

"I was a conscientious objector," he said, reading her mind correctly.

"And does your father consider that a debt he has to pay back as well?" she asked. After all, he had not hesitated to ask her personal questions.

"Not at all. Besides, I took care of my own debt. I worked in the Peace Corps for three years."

At that a natural silence seemed to fall, and Emma took the opportunity to glance at her watch. It was going on one o'clock. "I really should be on my way," she said, surprised that the time had passed so quickly.

He made no move to stop her now, standing up from the table to follow her out. "I'll see you to your car."

"There's no need for that."

"Are you kidding? With the crime rate around here?" he teased. "Have dinner with me tomorrow night? I mean, tonight?" he said, casually taking her arm as they walked through the lobby.

Emma stopped in her tracks. "What for?" she asked suspiciously.

Simon looked down at her in confusion. "How about because it might be fun?" he said, and then comprehension began to dawn. "Oh, you don't want me to pressure you about speaking at the dinner, do you? Well, I wouldn't do that. You said no and you sounded as if you meant it. No, I'm, uh, I'm looking at some real estate up here so I'll be staying for the weekend."

"Which agent are you using?" Emma asked, satisfied enough to resume her walk to the car.

"Which one do you recommend?"

"Well, I'd talk to Bonnie Morris if I were you. But don't you have an appointment with somebody?"

"Oh, do you need an appointment?" he asked. At that Emma glanced over at him, her doubts surfacing again, but he was the picture of uncalculated innocence. "Dinner?" he asked again as he held open the front door.

Emma considered. In her head she knew it wouldn't be very smart, but she decided to pay no attention to her head. "Okay," she said and then mentally chided herself on her lack of manners. "I'd love to," she amended.

"Good." He smiled. "Where do you live?"

She started to hesitate again, an old warning from her mother resurfacing after years of oblivion. Never tell a strange man where you live. "28 Maple Street, apartment 2," she said.

"I'll see you at eight?"

"We could have drinks there."

"Then I'll see you at seven-thirty." They had reached her car, Simon still holding her arm, and his grip on her elbow tightened as he started to turn her to face him. Some little demon gripped Emma at the last minute, however, and she turned her face so that his lips came down on her cheek instead of her mouth. He hesitated for a second and then kissed her chastely, but Emma could see out of the corner of her eye that he was smiling. "Good night, Emma," he said, amusement audible in his voice.

"Good night, Simon," she said, feeling silly. Well, she didn't want him to think she was too forward, did she? She stepped into her car and then rolled down the window and called out to him as he started walking back to the inn. "Simon?" He paused and turned. "What do you drink?"

"Scotch or bourbon."

"Well, which do you prefer?" she pressed. She had neither.

"I prefer scotch, Emma," he replied. He still sounded as if he were laughing, and she didn't see what was so funny now. She started her little red car and scooted down the driveway.

Emma managed to get through the first half of the next day as though it were a perfectly ordinary Friday. She found a coffee maker on sale, one that dripped through a filter into a very space-age looking thermos, and was so pleased with herself and it that she splurged on two new mugs with black and white cats on them. She started two loads of laundry and did her grocery shopping when they were in the dryer, with unusual efficiency. It was when she was on her way through town to the craft store, looking for a frame for some crewelwork she had just finished for her mother, that she walked past the dress shop.

Emma had never been into that shop before. Her work clothes rarely mattered, because she left most of the interviewing to Nora, one of her younger employees who happened to have a lot more poise in difficult situations than she did, and Emma was honest enough to admit it. She generally wore jeans or casual skirts and boots or sandals, peasanty clothes that she felt comfortable in and that suited her looks quite well. But the clothing in the little boutique she was eyeing speculatively was different, definitely "women's" clothing, and Emma suddenly realized that, literally, she did not have a thing to wear for the evening ahead of her. In fact, she had avoided thinking about it altogether. If it was still winter she might have managed with one of her nicer suits, but it was definitely spring and too late in the month for anything woolen.

She walked up the stairs and into the store rather hesitantly, pausing to inhale the hushed atmosphere redolent with some rich perfume. There was a young saleswoman seated behind a small, antique desk, idly leafing through a copy of *Vogue*, and she glanced up at Emma and then tactfully studied her for a moment. "May I help you?"

"I need a dress. Not terribly dressy, just something I can wear to dinner."

The saleswoman stood up with a satisfied expression on her face. "I have something that's perfect for you."

Twenty minutes later Emma left the store, trying to appear inconspicuous with a shimmering green bundle wrapped in plastic slung over her shoulder. The dress was, in fact, perfect for her. It was of a deep, moss-green silk, rather simply cut, as though the designer were aware that his fabric and her figure needed little else to be stunning together. It fell from softly padded shoulders to a waist that was cinched in with a wide belt, making the most of Emma's own slender waist and the smooth, full curve of her hips. The skirt was not terribly full and ended well below her knees. The neckline was high in the front, looking almost prudish, but then dipped a good eight inches in the back. She was a little nervous about that, but the saleswoman talked her into it. "You've got gorgeous skin. You should show it off," she said with finality. "Do you have any pearls? You'll need twenty four inches. We've got some nice-looking fakes here, if you don't."

Emma did have pearls. They were a gift from her grandmother when she got married. She did not, however, have the right shoes or purse, and the saleswoman was invaluable here as well. When she finally left she felt almost, but not quite, ashamed of herself.

She *needed* some real clothes, she told herself. On the other hand, once her date with Simon Eliot was over she would not have a single opportunity to wear them. That just meant that she would have to make sure she had a positively wonderful time, and then it would all be worthwhile. She was so absorbed in justifying her purchases that she forgot to walk home on the side of the street that did not pass in front of the Towne Restaurant, and as luck would have it, Stu was just leaving for her afternoon break as she reached the door.

"Get a load of you!" her friend exclaimed in a voice that suddenly seemed awfully loud. "I'm embarrassed just to look in the windows of that place, and you look like you just bought half the store."

"I did," Emma confessed sheepishly.

"What for?"

"I—have a date tonight."

"Emma, you're not going to waste that on Tony, are you?" Stu demanded.

"No, I met somebody." Stu waited patiently for the explanation, and Emma finally relented. She was bursting to talk about this, anyway. "Look, do you have time to come home with me? I want your opinion of this thing," she said, gesturing casually to the "thing" that had just cost her almost two hundred dollars. On sale.

Stu gave her a severe look. "I'll tell Gus that Marcy is having a crisis and I need an extra hour," she said before disappearing inside the restaurant. Emma sighed. Marcy was Stu's ten-year-old daughter and Emma sometimes thought Stu treated her daughter like a thirty-year-old woman and her friend like an irresponsible ten-year-old.

"So where did you meet him?" Stu asked once they were safely in Emma's apartment. They had walked home briskly, in total silence, as though this were, indeed, a crisis of earthshaking proportions.

"I met him for a drink last night," Emma said vaguely.

"Well, yeah, but I mean before that. He can't just call you out of the blue and say, 'Let's go have a drink.'"

She flushed guiltily. "Actually, that's kind of what happened."

"Emma, *what* do you mean?"

Emma was beginning to understand why Marcy was generally such a well-behaved kid for a precocious ten-year-old. It clearly wasn't easy to get away with much around her mother. "He called when I was doing the show last night," she mumbled as she bent over to give her fullest attention to a tag attached to the sleeve of her gown.

"And you went out with him?" Stu asked, her voice rising a little on each of the last three words.

"No! I mean, I met him at the Lyons Inn and I had a cup of tea, and he had a glass of milk, for heaven's sake, and it turns out he's a friend of Philip's and perfectly safe." For reasons she decided to analyze much later, Emma neglected to mention the real reason Simon had called.

"What's he do?" Stu asked, clearly not appeased.

"He's a television producer."

"Well, that's okay, but he sounds like another one of your famous losers. I mean, a glass of milk! You know, you shouldn't waste your time on people you don't find attractive. I don't mean Tony, Tony's okay, but who is this guy that he has to get your brother to get dates for him? If you're going out with him just because you feel sorry for him, you'll live to regret it."

By now Emma was giggling helplessly, both from nerves and from Stu's complete misinterpretation of the facts. "Stu, I promise you, I don't feel the least bit sorry for him. And just to make you feel better, he's quite attractive."

"What does he look like?"

Emma hesitated. "He's tall, dark and handsome."

"Honey, there's no such thing."

Emma, uncharacteristically, giggled some more. "He is. He has blue eyes."

"He's gay."

"Then why does he want to have dinner with me?"

"He's probably heard of your cooking and wants a free meal."

"I didn't even offer to cook," she said. "What's the matter with you, Stu? Isn't this the kind of thing you're always pushing me to do? Here I've gone and found some exotic man who promises to show me a good time, and you don't believe in him. What if he's like Peter Pan and disappears? Or was that Tinker Bell?" Her smooth, white brow furrowed in mock concentration.

"Oh, honey," Stu said, coming over and hugging her, ignoring the mossy sheath she was sliding over her head. "It's just that nobody's good enough for you, that's all. If he has nice blue eyes, he must be okay. My father has the nicest blue eyes I've ever seen." That bit of excess information was typical of the way Stu's mind worked, and Emma never dreamed of questioning her any more closely on her brand of logic.

"So what do you think?" she asked, stepping into the shoes, purse in hand and pearls around her neck.

"Ooo, Emma, that color is perfect on you. It's lovely, but isn't it a little long? Although if they're wearing them that way now—my God, Emma, there's no back!" she exclaimed, having halted in her circle of inspection.

"There's plenty of back, it just dips down a little," she denied hotly. "And there's nothing back there that he's not supposed to see, anyway. Why do I feel as if the spirit of my mother has suddenly entered the room. Mom? What possessed you to leave New York?"

"Okay, okay, but what happens when you lean over? Won't the whole thing just fall off in the front?"

"That's what shoulders are for, sweetie, but if it will make you feel better, I promise not to lean over too abruptly."

"Oh, Emma, you look...you look majestic."

She sighed. "Well, I suppose that's better than looking sweet. I'd *like* to look elegant and, what's that word, lissome?"

"You do look elegant. He won't be able to keep his hands off you." Stu gave her friend another searching look. "I hope you're prepared for that. Emma?"

By seven-fifteen that evening Emma had worked herself into such a dither that she did not know what she was prepared for, and she couldn't quite figure out why she was so nervous or what she expected out of the evening. She had mentally retraced her encounter with Simon the previous evening and decided he had been giving her mixed signals, seemingly interested in her for herself alone at first and then revealing the real reason he had called her. Of course, since she had refused with such finality, he couldn't expect her to change her mind, and therefore the dinner invitation must have been prompted by a sincere desire to spend time with her. It was still possible that he just wanted an eating companion, however, and thought of her as a buddy, the sister of his good friend, no one to take seriously. But since Emma's feelings about him were all too clear in her own mind, she felt she was still at a disadvantage. She was beginning to feel a littly silly in her alluring gown, and if Simon hadn't also made the appropriate preparations, she would be irrevocably humiliated. Not that he could possibly have taken the pains with himself that Emma had taken.

She had washed her hair, thought seriously about curling it and then decided to play it safe and let it fall in its own natural waves. She had steamed her perfect complexion over a pot of boiling water full of vile-smelling herbs until it was a hot, angry red and then had had to stand in front of the freezer until it had returned to close to its normal color. Her nose was still a little pink, but the pink didn't show up too much when the lighting was low. She had painted vicious red on her fingernails and then cleaned it all off again. And now she was standing in front of the mirror in bra and panties and slip, and if she put her dress on and sat down to relax, it would wrinkle. She considered her options, slipped it on anyway, added all her finishing touches, and then went over and stood quietly by the window and tried to do the deep-breathing exercises she was always coming across in magazines.

She was close to hyperventilation by the time Simon rang the bell, at precisely 7:32. "You're being ridiculous," she told herself as she took one more deep breath, and gave her head a casual toss as she went to let him in. He was wearing a dark blue business suit, a crisp, pale blue shirt and a narrow, striped tie; his face was clean shaven, his hair was combed smoothly, and he couldn't have looked more intimidating if he had tried. It didn't help that he looked a little nervous himself and gulped like a schoolboy while he stood silent for a moment to take in her appearance. Emma was beyond noticing anything besides her own heartbeat. "Hello," she said, still a little out of breath.

"Hi," he answered, and took a seat on the couch Emma gestured to, then looked up at her in strained silence.

She glanced at him curiously and then turned her back and went into the kitchen. "How do you take your Scotch?"

"Better make it straight," he answered in a strangled voice. "I like your dress." He would have liked it a lot better if it were hanging on a hanger and she were standing before him without anything on at all, he realized with a sudden rush, but he didn't know how to convey that at this point in their relationship without sounding crude.

"Thanks," she said with a quick smile. She bustled in with his drink and her own dry sherry, set out cocktail napkins, went back into the kitchen for nuts and some grapes in little bowls, and paused by the coffee table thoughtfully. She could have done this all in advance, but she had wanted to give herself something to do when he got there in case things were awkward, which they certainly were. Simon was drinking his Scotch as though he were parched, and that couldn't be good for his upcoming ulcers. "Would you like some olives? Or another drink? How about some milk?"

"Emma," he said, catching her hand and forcefully tugging her down beside him on the couch. "How about you stop fluttering around like some old lady with her favorite nephew?"

Emma blushed and her eyes fell. "I'm sorry," she said stiffly.

"No, I didn't mean it like that, I mean—" He stopped in obvious frustration. "Why don't we get out of here? This place is so damn cozy it makes me nervous."

Emma glanced around at the admittedly cluttered little sitting room, lovingly adorned with antique knick-knacks and cherished bits of embroidery. "I'm sorry you don't like my apartment," she said, growing huffy this time and standing up abruptly to get her coat.

"No, that's not what I mean," he said, standing up abruptly as well—so abruptly that his knees knocked against the coffee table and it crashed over onto the floor, breaking both of their glasses and one of the bowls holding the nuts. They stared at the mess in silence for a moment, and then Simon, who was holding Emma's wrist in a firm grip, sat down, pulling her down along with him. "I'm sorry."

"For what? It seems to me you've done *several* things since you came in that you might consider apologizing for," she said, rather annoyed.

"I'm sorry I'm being so clumsy. And I don't just mean physically." He grinned at her, and Emma felt herself warming toward him, felt herself positively melting for him. "I've got these enormous hands and feet and sometimes I lose track of them." She glanced down at the hand that still held hers and was reminded of a German Shepherd dog she had once known that had never quite grown into its feet either. She suddenly saw him as he must have been at the age of fifteen, physically too big for himself, and she didn't think he would intimidate her anymore.

"That's okay," she said, her voice getting soft and husky. Her hand was released, but before she had a chance to stand up, Simon's hand was resting heavily on the back of her neck, giving her tense muscles a gentle massage, and Emma remembered with a physical rush that he hadn't been fifteen years old for some time.

He moved closer, trapping her in the corner of the sofa with his looming body, and as his mouth came down toward hers, her head was effectively caught and held. He remembered her trick of the night before. That didn't matter. She had other tricks. "I should clean up that mess."

"Why?" he asked, his lips a half inch from hers.

"So that Percy won't, um, get glass in his paws," she replied with a gulp.

"Emma, do you have some objection to my kissing you?" he asked, his lips still hovering near hers.

"No, I guess not," she whispered.

"Because I think it might make us both feel a little less nervous. You know, we could sort of get it out of the way," he added persuasively.

"Yeah. All right."

"Good." He hesitated for one more second and then gently laid his mouth on hers, using his lips to urge her to open to him before inserting his tongue to taste her more fully.

Emma had not been thoroughly kissed in a long time, and she was shocked to hear herself gasp and feel her pulse start to race at the penetration of his tongue. Her confused senses tried to absorb everything at once: the sweet taste of the Scotch that still clung to his mouth, the glimmer of amusement in his half-closed blue eyes, the way his black hair feathered around the back of his ear. And then she gave herself up to the sensations caused by the warm moisture of his mouth, let her mouth respond to his without giving a second thought, licking his tongue, biting his lip and leaning back in his arms to allow his one free hand to trail up the silk of her dress to cover her breast.

When she felt her nipple budding into his palm through the insignificant fabric she gave a low, unconscious moan and arched her head back, and Simon took full advantage of her exposed, vulnerable flesh. His lips bit into the taut, white skin of her neck as he pressed her further back against the sofa, letting her feel the heavy force of his body weight while his palm continued to toy almost innocently with the contours of her ripe breast.

"Emma," he finally said, his breathing ragged and his heartbeat frantic just above hers. "Do you really want this to go on?"

"What?" His hand was still rubbing over her breast in a motion that he probably thought was soothing, but it was driving her nearly crazy, and she wondered if this was an example of his "losing track" of one of his extremities.

"Despite appearances to the contrary, I don't think you're ready to go to bed with me just yet, and although I'd be delighted to oblige you in any way that I could, you might not want to see me again, and I wouldn't like that. I meant that to be a simple, exploratory kiss. So why don't we just slow down?"

Emma sighed in frustration and finally grabbed at the offending hand. "Then stop it!" she said in exasperation.

He looked at his hand as though he had, in fact, no idea what had possessed it to behave in such a way, then sighed gustily, wrapped his arms around her pliant body, and gave her a rather fierce squeeze. "I'm sorry," he said when he finally looked up to meet her surprised expression. "I didn't mean to get carried away like that."

Emma didn't know what to say. She was painfully aware of the fact that she had been out of circulation for so long that she couldn't tell when someone was being sincere or just handing her a line. She had no idea if Simon only wanted to go to bed with her, if he wanted something more than that or if he merely wanted to be buddies. Her own feelings were in such a jumble that it would take quite a while to sort them out, and she was just wishing she had a prompter or something when help came from an unexpected quarter.

"You don't want to hear that now, do you?" Simon said, standing up with a sudden burst of energy and hauling her awkwardly to her feet. "You want me to stop wrinkling your dress and feed you, which is what the original agreement called for. So why don't you go put yourself back together while I try to clean up some of the mess I've made of your living room. You don't mind if the cat has a little of your sherry, do you?"

"Oh, Percy," she exclaimed, going onto her knees and starting to pick up the pieces of glass from the rug, where the cat was quietly and industriously licking the sherry from the sodden wool.

"It's okay, cats don't like glass," Simon informed her, watching her for a moment and then taking it upon himself to straighten her pearls, find her shoes and purse and smooth her hair.

Three

By the time they were sipping after-dinner brandies in Litchfield's finest restaurant, Emma had begun to feel at ease. While her share of the wine had certainly done its part in making her forget herself, Simon himself wasn't doing a bad job of drawing her out and charming her. He had carefully steered their way around the more traditional and mundane dinner conversation topics onto Emma's love for jazz, a subject which never failed to inspire her until her eyes sparkled and she ate without deliberately savoring every morsel. For a person as emotionally tied to good food as Emma, this was a rare feat.

After they had both virtuously declined dessert and then rewarded themselves with the brandy, Simon tactfully brought up the subject of Emma's marriage and her subsequent escape from New York. And Emma, warming to him, began to confide in him.

"It wasn't that I hated New York so much, just that everything I had taken for granted about myself suddenly just wasn't true. I can't be successful in the same way that my family is successful, and if I get involved in New York again I feel I might lose myself in the process, or lose what I've built up here. I guess that sounds a little strange to you," she said, staring at the glass she held in her palm and swirling the amber liquid.

"No, I don't think it's strange," he said, watching her watching the brandy. "I thought it was a little strange for you to turn my proposal down so fast last night."

As the meaning of his words penetrated Emma's fog of absorption, she developed a look on her face that could only be described as mulish. She tossed back the rest of her brandy and set the glass on the table with a careless shrug. "Well," she temporized, and then decided that was a good enough answer.

Her dinner companion did not agree. "Well?"

Emma sighed. "I won't change my mind," she warned. Simon nodded to show that he concurred with her terms. "Although I would have said no in any event, what made me angry was my brother's underhanded way of trying to get me back into that mess," she began, choosing to omit the other reason she was angry. "I'm making it on my own terms here and sometimes I suspect my family just can't accept that, and this proves it. Oh, they never actually come out and *say* anything, but I spent all those years hiding in my room listening to records while my brother and sister were out there turning into whiz kids, and I know they wondered what was wrong with me, why I wasn't like them. Now Philip thinks if I come back I won't be able to resist the lure of the Big Apple," she said with a sarcastic flourish. "But it won't work." She reached for her glass to punctuate her sentence and, seeing it was empty, set it back on the table with a slightly less self-confident gesture.

Simon watched the performance in silence, chin resting on his hand. When he was sure she was finished, he said, "But, Emma, Philip had nothing to do with my coming up here."

"You said that you play squash with him," she countered.

"I do. But he didn't send me up here to lure you back to New York. He happens to think you are terrific just the way you are. Don't you know that?"

Once again Emma decided she did not like the turn the conversation was taking. She couldn't imagine why she kept discussing things with Simon that she generally cared to discuss with no one but her cat. She felt a little like an adolescent whose emotions were always just under the surface, waiting to erupt, and she made a concerted effort to be much less personal. "So how did you and Phil become friendly?" she asked in a rather remote voice.

"We were both at the racquet club looking for a game at eleven o'clock one night," he said blandly, playing along with her. "We're pretty evenly matched. We've been getting together for a game a couple of times a week ever since."

"I see," she said. He didn't seem willing to offer more than that, so she had to resort to a bit of prodding. "And how did my name come up?"

"Oh, I happened to mention that we were having trouble finding somebody who knew enough about jazz to introduce Edmonds and he said it was too bad I couldn't get you to do it."

"Hmmm," she replied, not entirely convinced of her brother's innocence in the scheme.

"And when I started pressing for details he told me to leave you alone. He said you wouldn't do it and he didn't want me to pester you about it."

"Does he think I *can't* do it?" she asked, sitting up a little straighter.

"Emma, you can't have it both ways," he said, amusement blending with impatience. "Of course he thinks you can do it."

At that, even Emma had to laugh at herself a little.

"So will you do it?" he asked, pressing what he considered his advantage.

"No," she answered calmly, smiling at him. "I don't want to."

Simon opened his mouth to protest but could think of nothing to say in the face of that simple answer. "Well, shall we go then?" he finally asked.

"Thanks for dinner, it was delicious," Emma said when they were back in the car.

"It was my pleasure," he growled in response. Simon hated having the truth forced on him when it wasn't exactly what he wanted it to be, and he was decidedly miffed that he hadn't been able to charm his companion into obeying his wishes. He wasn't a bossy man; he was an idealistic one and had a certain selective blindness when it came to seeing things as he wanted them to be rather than as they often were. Up to this point the handicap had not seriously interfered with the success of any project he had undertaken, but Emma was posing a definite problem.

He was tempted to decide she was a worrisome pest and let it go at that until he happened to glance aside just as she was bending down to disentangle the seat belt. Her hair had parted over the nape of her neck, and eight inches of creamy velvet skin suddenly caught his attention. He took his hand off the key and remembered, with a certain tightening of his stomach muscles, exactly how he had felt about her dress when he had first seen her in it. One index finger, of its own accord, reached out and traced the line of her backbone down to the top of the shimmering silk. He wished she were naked.

Emma dropped the seat belt and sat up with a start. "Sorry," he muttered, turning his attention to starting the car. He would have to contend with Philip's anger enough as it was, without mauling his sister. He was going to take her straight home and get out of Litchfield in a hurry, and try to forget he ever came up. It was with very real surprise, therefore, that he heard himself saying, "How about going sailing tomorrow? I noticed signs for a Lake Waramaug on the drive up."

"Yes, that's just about twenty minutes away. But I can't sail," she confessed.

"Then you can go along for the ride and I'll do all the work. It's supposed to be nice tomorrow. Come on," he urged, giving her his most winning smile.

It was a combination Emma had no inclination to resist. "I'd love to," she admitted.

Simon was inordinately pleased. He was accustomed to women liking his company, but there was something about Emma that made it especially important that she like him, too. He decided it might be because he thought so highly of her brother.

When they reached her door, he said, "I'll pick you up around ten," and started to turn away, forgoing a goodnight kiss like the good brotherly figure he was trying to convince himself to be, but something in her demeanor stopped him. She hadn't made any move toward him, had even put the key in the lock, ready to turn it and go in, but he could tell she was waiting for him to kiss her.

He could also tell that if he left she wouldn't try to stop him. But she wanted him to kiss her. How could he disappoint her?

He turned back and took a half step toward her, slipping a hand lightly behind her back and bending down to brush her lips chastely with his, but when their mouths came together, he felt an impact on his senses that caught him completely off guard. Her lips were just barely parted and Simon couldn't stop himself from tasting them with his tongue, parting them a little further, delving into the welcoming moisture. Blood shot through his veins in a dizzying rush and he pulled her close in a convulsive grip, wrapping his other arm around her and half lifting her off her feet.

He could feel her shudder against him, feel her breath coming in quick, short gasps until she gave a weak little moan and reached up to put her arms around his neck. He realized she could barely stand, and with that realization came awareness that he wasn't sure he was doing the right thing and that, right or wrong, the hall was not a good place to do it in. Reluctantly he pulled his mouth from hers. "Emma," he whispered in her ear, still holding her close. "You'd better go inside."

"Right," she answered in a voice huskier than usual as she slowly began extricating herself from his arms. "I'll see you tomorrow," she said, giving him an unsteady smile and disappearing into her apartment.

Simon stared at the closed door for another minute before slowly going down the stairs. Several important factors were becoming clear. One of them was that Emma Beckett was not his typical choice for female companionship. He had never, once he outgrew a period of youthful awkwardness, lacked women friends, but those he chose to spend time with wanted the same things from a relationship that he did—friendship, respect, often intimacy, but no emotional demands, no old-fashioned illusions, no...romance.

He had realized after dinner that there was no chance of his getting Emma to change her mind about giving the presentation and what he realized now was that he was beginning not to care. But the main reason he had asked her to dinner in the first place was to see if he could make her change her mind, his comment about talking to a real estate agent being a complete fabrication. He didn't seriously believe in the word no. He would, of course, have been blind and deaf not to have realized she was attractive, but it had not been his original intention to mix pleasure with business. Somehow in the course of the evening, though, business had lost out entirely.

The thing that worried him now was that he sensed, looming on the horizon, a sticky situation, and the fact that he enjoyed, would like to continue enjoying, a friendship with Emma's brother was only one small part it. Simon had always blithely escaped falling in love, and this left him to direct his considerable energies to his professional life and to a wide assortment of hobbies. He had, in fact, always devoted an unusual amount of time to outdoor activities, of which sailing was only one. In his secret heart of hearts, he found it unpleasant going home to his empty apartment, so he solved that minor problem by spending as much time as possible keeping himself occupied outside it. It was when he had first seen Emma's apartment, lived in and loved and shared only with a cat, that he realized how different he and Emma were. She had something he hadn't realized he was missing, and although that thought made him nervous initially, he decided to proceed without worrying about it, the way he lived much of his life. He never let the inher-

ent danger in any given sport—skydiving, say, or downhill skiing—keep him from trying it, and it never
occurred to him that a woman like Emma could possibly
be any different from a particularly challenging slope.

As Simon was finishing his reflections and deciding to
forge ahead, Emma was sitting on her couch in the dark,
absently stroking Percy and covering her silk dress with
a fine film of cat hair. She had had a delightful evening,
notwithstanding its awkward beginning, and had enjoyed the rather unusual sensation of putting herself in
someone else's hands. She had felt Simon orchestrating
the evening, manipulating her, but she had not realized
to what extent she was letting him take charge until he
had more or less lost control of the situation and they had
both floundered into the unintentionally passionate kiss
at her door. It had begun when he had run his finger
down her back in the car, and she shivered a little at the
memory of his fleeting touch.

Emma had no doubts at all about Simon's basic worth
as a person or about his undeniable appeal. What she did
find disturbing was the ease with which she had surren-
dered to him, and she suspected that if he had wanted to,
he could have sweet-talked his way straight into her bed
and, consequently, into her life. Consequently for her,
anyway. Emma avoided physical entanglements because
she wanted to avoid the resultant emotional entangle-
ment that tended to disrupt her peaceful existence. Given
that basic philosophy, perhaps it wasn't wise to keep
seeing Simon, even if he was just up to look at real estate
and wanted to kill a little time.

She lifted the cat off her lap and went into her lighted
bedroom, seeing for the first time the gray fluff all over
her dress, and it did not occur to her to wonder when Si-

mon would get around to looking at property if he was taking her sailing.

Lake Waramaug was huge and beautiful, and was still glistening in the morning sun when Emma and Simon drove over the next morning. From a distance it looked calm and clear, but when they had parked Simon's dark gray Mercedes and walked down to the first boat house they came to, Emma could see that the water looked gray and a little wild as it beat rhythmically against the shore. The lake was the second largest natural lake in Connecticut, and nestled down between the mountains like a prize gem for anyone willing to drive the twisting road over from New Preston to find it.

While Simon negotiated the boat rental, Emma stood outside, soaking in the sunshine that was unusually warm even for late April. She had slept well the night before, and had enjoyed waking up to the feeling that she had something special to do that day. She was surprised that she had no desire whatsoever to back out of her date, but she hoped Simon would be willing to take everything fairly slowly, to keep things casual, and she decided not to worry about the vague future. Today would be much more relaxing than the night before—she could just wear jeans and a cotton sweater and look forward to having a good time.

When Simon appeared on the little dock with the proprietor and pointed out the boat he wanted, Emma took a minute to study him before joining him. He had told her last night that he was thirty-nine years old, but he looked younger. She could see a few gray hairs showing up among the black now that he was in the sunlight, and a few lines etched around his eyes and mouth, but his body was firm and athletic, and when she remembered how it had felt pressed against hers the night before, she felt herself beginning to flush. But she pushed that thought firmly out of her mind and went down to join him. She was determined not to spend the day gazing humbly at his body and then feeling too shy even to talk to him.

"You can swim, can't you?" he asked as he tossed a couple of stained orange life vests into the hull of a little yellow Sunfish.

Emma took in the situation in a glance. "Of course," she answered untruthfully. If she said no, she reasoned, he would try to make her wear one of those vests, and she would feel absolutely ridiculous. She was sure he was a perfectly adequate sailor, the sky was a clear, calm blue, and she decided on the spur of the moment that she would rather die with dignity than live and not look her best.

She let Simon help her into the bottom of the boat and then sat down abruptly as it dipped with his added weight. She immediately got the seat of her jeans wet, but as Simon gave one hearty push off the dock and then let the wind catch the sail, she forgot every minor discomfort as the little boat jumped ahead. The lake was big enough and open enough to have a fairly stiff wind, and Emma was amazed at the speed with which they approached the opposite shore. The sun was not quite hot enough to offset the cool breeze, but the feeling of physical delight that had possessed her when they first began moving increased with their speed.

She was feeling the first tingle of alarm at the rapid approach of the opposite shore when Simon bent down to her. "I'm going to bring her around. Get ready to duck...now!" She crouched over in the seat as he swung the sail over their heads; the boat heeled sharply, spraying them with water, and then took off in the opposite direction like a spirited horse. She looked up to laugh with him and found him surprisingly near.

"Do you like it?" he asked.

"It's wonderful!"

"Why don't you get up here beside me and I'll show you how to do it."

Emma hesitated only for an instant before scrambling over to the narrow ledge to sit beside him. He smiled down at her, looking awfully pleased with himself before starting the lesson. "This stick back here controls the rudder, which you turn in the opposite direction from the one you want to go in, like this. Put your hand on it," he ordered, and when she obeyed he let go. "When we go back and forth like this we're tacking, because with the wind from the west we can't just go straight out into the lake. Now, in just a minute I'm going to bring the sail back around and you turn the rudder," Emma nodded her acceptance of this proposal, intent on watching for his signal and feeling the weight of the water against her hand. "All right, let's try it now," he said when they were still a good fifty yards from the shore. He pulled on the line attached to the sail as Emma pushed the rudder over to the other side; the boat turned abruptly, and the boom swung around, giving her a gentle clap on the side of her bent head and provoking a graceless entrance into the dark, chill water.

It took Emma a moment or two to figure out what had happened, and by the time she opened her eyes and looked around, she was completely disoriented and could not figure out which way was up. Her first coherent thought was that it was so easy not to do anything. She felt terribly heavy and she knew that if she did nothing she would die. It was when she thought about her obituary that she saw the absurdity of the situation. Killed by her own passivity, it would read, and Emma suddenly thought that that did not suit her at all. She gave a furious kick, and when the world around her gradually began to grow a little lighter, she gave another one. And then, to her surprise, her head shot above the water and she saw Simon standing up in the boat, holding the crumpled sail in one hand and looking around wildly. He was already about twenty yards away, and it took another second or two for him to spot her, but Emma was tired from her exertion and felt fatalistically that the decision was out of her hands.

She could see the relief in his face as soon as his eyes found her. "Just tread water, I'll come get you," he called out across the distance, sitting back down in the boat and starting to paddle to her with the emergency oar. "I thought you weren't going to come up," he said, intent on his task.

Tread water? Emma thought. What the hell? Her feet made a curious stepping motion that seemed like a tread to her, but her body's natural tendency was to sink, and there didn't seem to be anything she could do about it. She looked at Simon reproachfully, but he still seemed much too far away, and she started to go back under water, dimly aware of his voice calling her name and cursing in the distance. She was fully aware of what was happening this time, and rather than feeling silly, she was suddenly furious about it. She was going to die because she had been vain. It seemed like much too harsh a punishment for such a stupid crime, but it was happening. She flailed her hands in a sudden frenzy but it didn't help, and when her hair was suddenly caught in something, she knew with a suffocating fear that she was finished.

She was doubly surprised, therefore, when the pressure on her hair increased and her head was suddenly, roughly, jerked back above the water and she found herself gazing into a pair of blue eyes that were narrowed against the sunlight. "I thought you could swim," she heard a voice say. Speech was still beyond her, but she shook her head slowly, hanging limply from his hand and closing her eyes when the expression in his evolved into one of fury, and he uttered a string of curses. When she decided it was safe, she opened her eyes again and reached up to put her arm around his neck, but he snapped, "Let go!" and then turned her roughly around to insure that she did. He put one arm across her chest, gripped her under her arm and began hauling her back to the boat with a few firm, swift strokes. When they reached it, he pushed her up against the side, curtly ordered her to hold on, and then pulled himself aboard. By now Emma was hoping he would just paddle away and leave her to drown in peace, but he leaned over and pulled her up by the waistband of her jeans, letting her sprawl unceremoniously across his lap while he pulled the sail in and paddled back in to the boat house.

Emma managed to slide off his lap and huddle in the bottom of the boat, trying to cough discreetly. The water had been a lot more welcoming than Simon, and she was still sufficiently miserable to be a little sorry he had rescued her. After all, he would probably have been plagued with guilt for the rest of his life if she had died, and the thought of his being miserable for any reason was very appealing. All too soon, however, he was maneuvering the boat up to the dock and expertly tying it up.

As soon as it was possible, Emma stood up stiffly and stepped onto the dock, refusing to look at Simon and walking up to the street and over to the car with as haughty a posture as she could manage. She stopped short of actually getting in the car, however, knowing that her soaked clothing would not do the leather upholstery any good and wishing she were inconsiderate enough not to care. When Simon joined her she was leaning against the car, hoping vainly that the sun would get a little warmer. The day, with spring fickleness, had begun to turn cooler, and she was holding herself stiffly in order not to shiver too violently.

Simon's temper didn't appear to have abated at all. He didn't say anything at first, silently taking off his work shirt and wringing it out, then yanking open the back door of the car and tossing it onto the floor. When he finally faced her, planting himself before her aggressively with his arms crossed on his bare chest, she felt a quiver of alarm in the pit of her stomach. "Just tell me one thing," he began in a deceptively calm voice. "Why did you do that? I've never met a first-class idiot before and I'm curious."

Emma felt a few tears begin to well up and she closed her eyes in order to contain them. She had nothing to say to this horrible man, and all she wanted was to go home, take a hot bath and crawl into bed. Besides, if she actually did try to talk, she was fairly certain she would start to cry, and he would probably think she was crying because he was being mean, and she refused to give him that satisfaction.

"Why did you tell me you could swim?" Simon asked insistently. "And why didn't you wear one of those life jackets? You saw me put them in the boat." Emma opened her eyes and looked at him, then looked steadily away, trying to appear bored. "Dammit, answer me!" he snapped furiously and at that Emma answered him. Without giving the matter any thought at all, she took one step toward him and gave him a swift right hook on the chin. He tried to jerk his head away but the blow connected, and when he regained his balance, a curiously glazed look in his blue eyes, he found Emma turning away from him to lean on the car and cry into her hands.

He took her arms, gently this time, and helped her into the back seat of the car, sliding in beside her and pulling the door shut. "Emma," he growled in her ear, hugging her tightly against his bare chest and imprisoning her arms between them. "You scared me to death."

"Well, how do you think I felt, you big jerk?" she said in a shaky voice and then sobbed without restraint, pulling her arms free and wrapping them around his neck.

His hold on her changed somehow then. It couldn't have gotten any tighter, but he held her against more of his body, and she became aware of his slightly roughened chin against the skin beneath her ear and the damp curls of hair on the heated wall of his chest. "I'm sorry," he whispered, his hot breath warming her ear as his hand slid down her back to lightly caress her hips through her wet jeans and then press her against him. Emma felt his own urgent need, felt that the atmosphere in the car was suddenly charged with desire, and when his hand came up to cup her chin and tilt her head back so that he could find her mouth, her lips were already parted and ready to receive him.

He groaned softly when his tongue met her own unresisting one, when she let him stroke and become familiar with all the sensitive parts of her mouth. He pressed her back onto the seat, his kiss deepening and becoming more demanding, and with a low whimper she began to meet his demand, responding to his mouth with her lips and teeth, running her hands over the bare flesh of his back and then up to caress the back of his neck. Emma felt the blood pounding in her veins with uncharacteristic force, heating her entire body, and when she felt Simon draw away from her long enough to pull her sodden sweater off over her head, she helped him, arching her back while his hand fumbled with the hook of her bra.

She lay back, naked from the waist up, her arms flung wantonly over her head while his eyes drank in the sight of her. And then with another moan of capitulation he lowered his head and ran his tongue over each soft breast, glorying in the taste of her abundant flesh, sucking each tightening peak that pointed at him with a demand of its own. When he lowered his bare chest onto hers, she felt a wave of need course through her lower body, and she arched her hips into his with a shudder. "Simon," she whimpered in his ear, completely overcome by her own desire.

"I want to make love to you," he whispered against her neck, and she tilted her head back to enjoy more fully the delicious tingle caused by his breath on her skin. It was when the tingle died away, when she noticed he had become rather still, as though he were waiting for her to answer him, that she realized what he had said, realized she was lying in the back seat of a car, topless, on the verge of giving herself to a man she had known less than forty-eight hours.

"Oh my God," she said, suddenly feeling rather chilly but hesitant to press any closer to the nearest source of warmth.

"Not here, Emma," he said, having the audacity to look amused. "We'd probably be arrested."

"No" was her only answer.

"You don't think so? Well, I'm game if you are."

"I mean *no*," she said, feeling a powerful urge to hit him again. "I mean, where's my shirt? Take me home."

Simon sat up slowly and felt around on the floor of the car until he found her sweater, still soaking wet and covered now with dirt and grit. His own shirt was a little better, however, and he stepped outside and shook it vigorously before getting back in and handing it to her. "Put this on," he said quietly.

She pulled it around her tiredly and then leaned back in the corner of the seat, feeling miserable. He gently buttoned it shut and reached across her to open the door. "Get in the front seat." Emma silently obeyed, willing now to let him take charge. Obviously she could trust him more than she could trust herself. She didn't want to talk and he seemed to sense that, letting her lean back in the seat and stare at the passing countryside in silence as he drove back to Litchfield.

It wasn't until they reached the outskirts of town that he spoke. "Are you going to be all right? You must have swallowed some water back there."

"I'll be fine," she answered quietly. The truth was that physically she didn't seem to have suffered any mishap at all.

After riding on in silence for another moment or two, he pulled up and stopped in front of the big old white house where she lived. She started to gather her things and get out, but he stopped her with a hand on her arm. "Listen, I'm sorry I yelled at you back there. I was pretty shaken up, but I should have realized you were more so."

"That's all right," she said stiffly, wanting nothing now but to get out of the car and be away from him. "I don't see a place to park, but if you want to wait here I'll bring your shirt back to you."

"No, that's okay, just hold on to it." He paused for a moment and then continued, staring straight ahead, his eyes narrowed as if in concentration. "I have plans for dinner, and I've got to drive back to New York early tomorrow, but...I'll be seeing you, okay?"

"Okay, Simon," she said, irritated with him now for feeling the need to lie. When, exactly, would he be seeing her? But she supposed it wasn't smooth simply to say goodbye. "And thanks for taking me sailing."

She climbed out of the car, but distinctly heard the note of amusement in his voice when he answered, "It was my pleasure, Emma."

Once in her apartment she sat down heavily on the couch, heedless of the wet stain from the seat of her pants. How, she wondered, had everything gone downhill so fast? Simon had certainly not been particularly nice, considering the fact that she had almost drowned, and she strongly suspected it was something specific that had caused him to drive away with a careless "I'll be seeing you." She didn't think he liked her as much as he had seemed to at first, but she couldn't tell when his feelings had begun to change.

She supposed it was true some men had no use for a woman who wouldn't go to bed with them right away, and from the circumstances here it was possible he was like that. But Emma was a fairly good judge of character and she didn't think Simon was that shallow. No, something else must have happened to turn him off.

She sighed and went into the bathroom to peel away her clammy clothes and fill the tub with hot water. On impulse she added some lavender bubble bath, knowing she needed to feel loved and pampered, if only by herself. It didn't actually matter, anyway, why Simon had so clearly pulled away from her. She didn't want a relationship with a man, didn't want the emotional intrusion, didn't want to change any of her comfortable, solitary ways. What really rankled, she forced herself to admit, was that she liked to think she lived the way she did by choice. She liked that feeling of having the world at her doorstep and saying no. And now she had met somebody who said no first. It was galling.

Did she really like Simon that much? She found him disturbingly attractive, she thought, and then, relaxing against her bubbles, subjected herself to a severe cross-examination. Why was that so disturbing? Why had she been so dead set against making love to him this afternoon? Wasn't that preferable to a solitary bubble bath? Ah, but that would have required some risk on her part, and Emma hadn't had any risk in her relationships with another human being in years. Her friendship with Stu had always been easy and natural. They liked each other's company, had long, meandering discussions about everything and nothing; but Stu's primary emotional commitment was to her daughter, and Emma found that strangely comforting. And Tony was simply, well, there. She had always been happy to have him there, but he had long ago accepted the fact that they would never be more than buddies. Emma used to tell herself that she had avoided letting their relationship become sexual because that would have caused Tony to become too attached to her, but she was beginning to suspect differently now. Not only was there some elemental spark of attraction missing, there was also some elemental fear in herself.

It wasn't entirely fear, however, that had made her withdraw from Simon in the car that afternoon. She supposed that over the years she had become emotionally lazy. She asked very little from her friends, and while she herself was a warm and supportive employer and a sympathetic and supportive friend, not a single person in Litchfield was entirely in her confidence. She wasn't ever cold, but there were certain barriers in her psyche that she wouldn't take down for anybody.

Emma was aware of this quality but she did not see it as a flaw. When she had been going through her divorce she had had to concentrate all her energy on being strong, and at the time being strong had meant keeping her feelings to herself. Although she tended to gravitate toward Stu when she was feeling depressed, it would never have occurred to her to sit down and unburden herself completely. She and her cat were sufficient unto themselves.

Her family, of course, was another matter entirely. Sometimes she felt as though she were deliberately hoarding her nurturing instincts for the few times a year when they came up, singly or together. Emma was by unspoken consensus the maternal element in the family and loved nothing better than to gather them all into her tiny apartment and fill them with holiday cooking. She was the only Beckett with a shred of domesticity, and they adored her for it and drew on it freely. The four members of her immediate family, however, were the only people in the world who were always welcome to do so.

The fact that her brother apparently thought well of Simon was a good recommendation, but Emma was still not inclined to risk her peace of mind by getting involved with him. He was a dynamic individual but he wasn't her type. His behavior after she turned him down in the car was proof of that, wasn't it?

By now the water was getting cold and she had had enough of sitting around by herself and probing her conscience. She wrapped herself up in a warm robe, fixed a cup of hot tea and sat down to call Tony. The fact that

Simon had apparently had enough of her company was
no reason to sit around and mope.

It was four-thirty in the afternoon, and she was surprised to learn that Tony had left the Ranger Station for
the day. "Yup," his boss informed her. "Asked for time
off to get a trim and pick up a new suit. I figured you two
have something pretty special planned for tonight, huh?"

"Sure do, George," she said, finding it easier to play
along. She, for example, planned to go to the drugstore
and buy the trashiest novel she could find, then pick up
a little bottle of Grand Marnier and settle down for a very
special evening all by herself. "Just let him know I called
if he checks in, will you?"

Emma had first met Tony when she had taken Stu's
daughter, Marcy, then four years old, to a "My Wood-
land Friends" program sponsored by the parks depart-
ment. Tony had guided their troop on a nature walk and
he had immediately been drawn to the rambunctious
child and the pretty woman he assumed was her mother.
Emma had suspected at the time that he was misled, but
she had found his easy friendliness, void of any sexual
innuendo, a comfort, and she hadn't clarified her relationship with Marcy. She ran into him occasionally in
town after that, let him carry her groceries home once,
gave her opinion on wallpaper he was selecting for his
bathroom when he spotted her in the hardware store; and
when her marital status gradually came to light, the pattern for their friendship had been set.

Tony had attempted, casually at first and then with
increasing ardor, to change the nature of their relationship, but Emma had found it easy to discourage him.
They were familiar enough that she could turn him down
without upsetting him too much, and good enough
friends that he didn't want to lose her by being too per-

sistent. Every now and then it would occur to him to press his suit again, but Emma suspected those incidents arose partly from boredom and partly from curiosity.

It was ironic that when he finally met Marcy's real mother, who was as available as Emma, neither one had been interested in the other. Emma had no matchmaking instincts, and while she would have been happy for them if they had fallen in love, she preferred to have her friends in two largely different spheres. Besides, if either of them married, she reasoned, they wouldn't need her as badly.

All the same, she was pleased that Tony had apparently found somebody worth buying a new suit for. She didn't think she had ever seen him in anything but blue jeans, but then she would have felt a little nervous if she had. She wondered just what he and his newfound friend were going to do. She doubted he would go in for pizza and a movie, and she didn't think he had ever set foot inside Sherman's, where Simon had taken her last night.

She stood up and hastily began pulling on some dry clothes. Despite her efforts to control her thoughts, they kept returning to Simon. She supposed there was no way to avoid that for the next day or two, simply because he was the most interesting thing to happen for some time, but she didn't have to wallow in remorse. She would just have to make a special effort to keep busy.

Seven hours later Emma threw the paperback across the room, where it hit the wall with a solid thwack. Percy raised his head and glared at her from the nest he had created between her feet, and then rested his chin comfortably on her ankle, closing his winking green eyes, not terribly impressed by his mistress's temper tantrum. The spy had finally realized that the woman he was in love with was not a traitor, but it was too late. She had already been killed by the Russian agent and it was partially his fault. Emma was furious. She had been counting on a happy ending, would not have bought the book if she had known True Love did not triumph. If you couldn't believe that Love would conquer All, what was there left to believe in?

She twisted around to fluff up her pillow and then settled down in bed, dislodging the cat, who circled around at the foot of the bed until he could regain his spot comfortably. She left the light on and stared up at the shadows on the ceiling, curiously keyed up and knowing she was destined to toss and turn for a while. She always got very involved in fiction, too involved, and was at the moment still too caught in the emotional turmoil of American Agent Race McShane to absorb the oddity that there was a hailstorm attacking only one of her windows. She lay still for another moment, listening to the persistent patter, and finally decided to get up to investigate.

She tossed aside the covers and padded to the window in her nightie, ignoring the furious Percy, who decided to deny her the pleasure of his company for the night and stalked from the room, tail held high. She leaned her forehead against the pane, trying to focus in the dark, but the reflection from the light behind her made it impossible to see and she finally opened the window and knelt down to peer out. There, standing below her, was Simon Eliot, emptying the pebbles from his pockets.

"Hello?" she called out uncertainly. "What are you doing?"

"Were you asleep?"

"No."

There was a moment of silence. "I came back for my shirt," his voice finally floated up. He sounded a little uncertain himself.

"It's probably still damp. I was going to wash it first, God knows why," she added in an undertone.

"Can I come up?"

She waited a moment before answering, as though she had to think about it. "Okay. The front door's locked by now. Just ring number two and I'll buzz you in." He disappeared around the corner of the house and she debated quickly whether or not she wanted to put on her robe. Her gown was long and modest, and her robe was pink and fuzzy and she felt as though it made her look fat. For the second time that day she let vanity win. At least the only thing she risked this time was a chill.

Four

Emma pressed the buzzer to unlock the downstairs door and then opened her own door and propped a shoulder against the jamb, waiting for him to climb the stairs. He took them two at a time and arrived before her in an instant, towering over her with a curiously bright look in his eyes. She wondered for a moment if he had been drinking with his dinner, but he didn't smell of liquor and he seemed perfectly steady on his feet. Silently, she took a step back and motioned him in.

"What are you doing?" he asked.

"Just reading in bed."

"You look like you're freezing. Why don't you go get back under the covers? I just want to talk to you for a minute."

Emma had indeed crossed her arms over her chest, but it wasn't because of the chilly spring night so much as because she decided her nightgown was not that modest

after all. It was a long flannel gown studded with faded
rosebuds, but it was thin after years of wear and she
wondered how much of her was visible through the fabric. She turned off the light in the sitting room abruptly
and went back to her bedroom, where she sat down and
pulled the covers way up, resting her chin on her knees.
She had no idea what Simon wanted, but he seemed perfectly at ease following her in and sprawling on his back
at the foot of her bed, apparently unmoved by whatever
he had managed to see or not see. Well, he had already
had one good look at her breasts—perhaps that was
enough.

Simon gazed at the ceiling in silence for a long moment, during which Emma gazed at him, trying to be
dispassionate about the way his suit jacket fell back to
reveal his firm stomach muscles, the way his hair needed
her hand to smooth it down, the way his eyes were bright
with concentration on something beside herself. Finally
he spoke. "I want to know why you didn't put on the life
vest."

Emma made an irritated little noise and shifted uncomfortably, not at all willing to tell him. He turned his
head and looked straight at her, subjecting her fully to his
piercing blue gaze for the first time that night. "Tell me,"
he said insistently.

"I just didn't want to," she muttered with a shrug of
her shoulders, feeling small and hoping he would be satisfied with her silly reason and go away.

"Emma, you almost drowned," he said, sitting up now
but not moving any closer.

"I know."

He gave her a long, considering look and she had to
fight an impulse to duck her head under the covers and
hide. "You sure don't seem very upset about it."

"Well, of course I was upset about it," she said defensively. "What are you getting at, anyway?"

Simon turned his gaze back to the ceiling. "Never mind," he said after a long silence.

"Listen, if you came here to get after me, why don't you just get it off your chest?" she asked, stretching a leg down and nudging him through the blanket with her toe. "Everybody I know gets around to it eventually."

"What do you mean?"

"The way I live tends to bother people," she explained, choosing her words with care. "You've already compared me to a little old lady with her favorite nephew."

Simon was growing increasingly uncomfortable. "That's not what I wanted to talk about," he said shortly, and then sighed. He had been sighing a lot lately. "The way you live doesn't bother me, although I admit I find it a little...frustrating. But I can't help wondering if the reason you pass up a lot of opportunities is that you're afraid. Because anyone as beautiful and intelligent as you should never be afraid."

He made the above speech to the ceiling rather than to her, and Emma was glad he wasn't able to see the expression on her face. At first she wasn't sure if he was talking about anything besides the invitation to speak in New York. She decided to deal with the least important point he had made. "I wasn't intelligent enough to finish college," she told him for the second time.

"No, but you could have. And having a degree doesn't mean you're smart. I have two, and most of the time I feel like a complete idiot," he finished with an irresistible grin.

Emma didn't have anything to say to that. She felt subdued and chastened, and she turned her head sideways to gaze out the black window and avoid having to look him in the face, having to answer him when she couldn't even answer herself. She had no idea at this point if what he said was true. Other people had scolded her periodically for isolating herself, for being too negative. Why did it matter so much more coming from him, when she barely knew him? Why did she let him do it? Who was he, anyway, this big, admittedly clumsy man, who sprawled across her bed as if he had a right to, criticizing her life? Her existence had always been so tidy and satisfactory, and now it was somehow awry, full of questions and vague dissatisfactions. She sighed heavily and looked back at him to find him still watching her.

"I want to be friends with you, Emma," he told her quietly. "And I don't like to see one of my friends not being fair to herself."

"Maybe you're the one that isn't being fair," she said, half to herself. "But I suppose we can be friends anyway."

He gave her a small smile and reached out to clasp her foot through the covers. "Why, thank you."

Emma wanted to smile back, wanted to take this all very lightly, but she had a curious feeling in her stomach and she couldn't seem to take her eyes off his face. He needed a shave. She wanted desperately for him to kiss her, could not believe she had actually avoided kissing him the night before, making love to him this afternoon. He had been ready to give her a wonderful gift and she had turned it down without a thought. It was a common failing of hers, to pass up golden opportunities and then be sorry forever. She wasn't about to make any kind of move toward him now, not after he had just finished telling her he wanted to be friends. She wasn't sure exactly what he meant by that, but finding out would involve too much risk. So instead she sat there, dry-eyed and still, while he looked at her with an amused, almost fond, little quirk to his lips, his hand still resting on her foot. It was one of those fragile moments that stretched into something permanent, that took on significance for no apparent reason.

"Well," he finally said. "I'd better get back to the hotel."

"Okay," she said, pushing the covers aside and standing up.

"Why don't you stay in bed? I'll let myself out."

"That's okay." It seemed to be her only word tonight. Okay. But was anything okay? She trailed along behind him through the darkened living room, shivering in earnest now, without a thought for the relative decency of her nightie. She was too confused to worry about details.

"I'll call you this week," he said when he reached the door.

She tried to think of an appropriate reply that didn't sound too passive. "I'd like that," she finally said.

"Good night."

"Good night." She locked the door behind him and hurried back to bed, curling up into a ball and hugging herself tightly. He had not touched her once, and she had desperately needed it. She didn't want to think about what he had said, didn't want to remember how it had felt to be under the water that afternoon and to know she was going down. If Simon hadn't been so quick to jump in and save her she would be dead now, she thought, forcing herself to confront the import of that possibility. She had not known what to do to save herself.

She had always felt perfectly content with her life, or at any rate had never felt particularly dissatisfied. She had struggled desperately as soon as she had realized she was really going under. And what about saying no to Simon, on both counts, out of fear? That was certainly the main reason she hadn't wanted their involvement to go any further, but was it also true for the presentation this summer? Did she get another chance at either? And did she want one?

She lay awake until dawn trying to figure herself out, and came to no overwhelming conclusions. She did decide that she was certainly glad Simon had pulled her out of the lake when he did, because there were a lot of things she still wanted to do. When she finally drifted off to sleep she had an almost peaceful look on her face, but there was something nagging at her, some little worry that she had not resolved. She fell asleep, however, without ever remembering that Simon had forgotten his shirt.

Simon, tossing in too short a bed at the Lyon's Inn, was not sleeping peacefully at all. He was coming to the unpleasant conclusion that he had been totally unjustified in barging in on Emma's mental state that way, making her question her motives, even her happiness. Viewed objectively, she seemed to have her life figured out quite well, and although she apparently had no desire to speak at the dinner and hadn't jumped at the chance to get involved with him, neither one was any reason to question the foundations of her existence. It was true she seemed to want him to call her, but it was also possible that she was simply being polite, and at this point he did not trust his own perceptions.

The real problem, he finally admitted to himself, turning on his side and watching with resignation as the sun finally rose, was that he envied Emma and he wanted Emma and he didn't know what to do about it. He decided that when he got home he would get very involved

in something and see if he could shake this not quite
pleasant feeling. Unfortunately he was afraid it was a little more tenacious than a bad cold.

"Well, Emma, why on earth *didn't* you wear the life
jacket?" Stu asked, fixing her with a disapproving look
over the top of her coffee cup. They were eating Sunday
brunch at a table in the corner of the Towne Restaurant's kitchen, a pleasant habit that had become a rit-
ual. The actual paying guests helped themselves to a
buffet brunch, which Stu leisurely replenished as the
spirit moved her. Her rationale was that on Sunday
morning people wanted to move at a slower pace and
didn't mind waiting twenty minutes for Stu to get around
to noticing the scrambled eggs were all gone. Once a
tourist had had the audacity to poke his head in the
kitchen to request fresh rolls and had come as close to
being tarred and feathered and run out of town on a rail
as anyone in recent history. Stu's position in Litchfield
was that of a firm but loving mother, and people found
themselves doing what she told them to in the belief that
it was for their own good. And now Emma, here, was
getting a little out of hand. She narrowed her eyes, in
her best don't-think-you-can-pull-the-wool-over-*my*-eyes-
young-lady look, and watched her friend squirm in her
chair uncomfortably.

"All right," Emma finally answered. "I didn't wear it
because I would have looked silly in it."

"Saints preserve us! Emma," Stu said, putting her cup
down abruptly enough to slosh coffee over the side. "Do
you know what I would do to Marcy if she did something like that? I would…I would *kill* her."

"Well, that would kind of defeat the purpose,
wouldn't it?" Emma replied. "Stu, I'm not Marcy. If I

was I wouldn't have this problem. Marcy would look sweet in one of those little orange vests. I would look like an army tank."

"So you'd let a little vanity determine whether you live or die?"

"There's nothing little about it. You see these breasts?" she said, leaning back in her chair slightly and displaying them to an advantage most men would have found irresistible. Stu was unmoved. "Can you imagine what they would look like covered by three inches of foam rubber?"

"Emma, I hate to shatter your illusions, but they're really not so enormous," her friend said acidly. "I mean, they don't precede you into every room. They're not the first thing people notice about you." She couldn't resist adding, "They're probably the second thing, though."

Emma looked as though she were about ready to throw the rest of her eggs at Stu. "You don't understand," she began, but Stu interrupted her.

"I'll let you in on a little secret, honey. Men like women's breasts." She paused as if to let her startling information sink in. "You know, if you'd worn that little vest and it bulged out all over the boat, Simon would probably have been so excited thinking about what was underneath it that he wouldn't have been able to sail."

"I don't think he's that impressionable." Emma muttered. She hadn't filled her friend in on anything that had happened after she had been hauled out of the water, partly because she couldn't stand to think about it, much less hear someone else's reaction. She sat back in her chair and waited while Stu went into the dining room to perform a few of her duties. It was a perfect day outside, and she could not think of a single thing she wanted to do. She tried to think of what she normally did on Sundays—read the paper, talked to Stu, took walks if it was nice, dropped by the studio to make sure everything was running smoothly. She rarely worked on weekends, letting her employees do the live shows and running taped "History of Music" programs. If anything was happening in the community that was controversial, she would have a call-in discussion program on Sunday night so that people could air their opinions, but she could not think of a single thing that needed discussion at the moment. She heaved a hearty sigh. What was the matter with her? She had no enthusiasm for anything. Had her life always been so dull?

Stu came back and settled into her chair with a smile lingering on her face. She had a good time at work, joking around with her regular customers, twisting her boss, Gus, around her little finger, hearing the intimate details of the lives of half the town. Oddly enough, she was the soul of discretion, which was why people tended to tell her so much. She looked up at Emma, still visibly drooping, and felt a rush of affection. "So when are you going to see this guy again?"

"I don't think I am. He...wasn't pleased with my behavior yesterday."

"He wanted to move a little too fast for you, huh?"

Emma pulled herself up from her slouch and stretched languidly, and then gave a shake of her head that looked as though she were trying to shake out bad thoughts. "That's only part of it. We're just not suited to each other, I think. I don't have anything to do today. Does Marcy want to go out and play with her Aunt Emma?"

It was an obvious change of subject, but Stu didn't press her. "I'm sure Marcy would love to play with Aunt Emma. Unfortunately she has to finish her three-dimensional map of Italy this afternoon or she won't be allowed to watch *The Wizard of Oz* on television to-night.''

"You would do that?" Stu nodded decisively. "What a mean mom. Can I go help her build Italy?"

"You can do the whole thing for her, if you want. Why don't you let her rehearse her oral report on you, too? She could use a public-speaking lesson from a professional."

"I'm not much of an example. The only audience I can talk to without getting nervous enough to wet my pants is a microphone."

When Emma reached Stu's house, the radio was blaring (playing her station, at least), the kitchen table was littered with several large pieces of cardboard, a fine coating of flour, and pots and paint, and Marcy was just taking her first batch of chocolate chip cookies out of the oven. The ten-year-old was a divine and dedicated baker of desserts, and Emma eyed her whippet-thin body enviously for a moment. She liked to cook quite a bit herself, and the two of them often spent an afternoon concocting complicated dinners for Stu and Tony, neither of whom was a very appreciative consumer. "I didn't know Italy was made out of cookies," she mused, propping herself against the door jamb.

"Oh, hi, Emma," Marcy said, guiltily licking some chocolate off her fingers. "See, I was just getting started, and I made up this clay out of flour and water and salt, and it reminded me that I hadn't made any cookies for a while. Want some?"

"I'd love some, but I want to be able to leave through the same door I came in by, so I'd better not."

"You're not fat. You know who's fat? This girl in my class named Delphine. God, she's *so* fat." Marcy spread her arms to indicate an impossibly wide girth, mainly to

distract her mother's friend from the fact that she hadn't
been doing what she was supposed to be doing.

"Well, it's a good thing Delphine's not here, or she'd
eat up all your cookies. Do you want some help on your
map or have you decided not to do it and hope that no
one will notice?"

"Will you help me? See, I don't know what Italy looks
like."

"Try looking at a map, Marcy. Do you have an atlas
or an encyclopedia?" She nodded. "Run and get it. We
can put the coloring right in the clay and then just throw
it together. It won't take long."

It took a lot longer than Emma had hoped it would.
She had forgotten what an irritation junior high school
could be, and how many contours and convolutions there
were in the geography of Italy. Marcy considered con-
structing tiny little cities all over the country, but settled
on a major landmark for each major city, and did not
even try to make tiny little people to scatter on the
beaches. Emma concentrated on getting the proper lean
to the Tower of Pisa and let Marcy work on a rather
crude Colosseum and the Ponte Vecchio.

When Italy was put into the refrigerator to harden, she
listened to Marcy's five-minute report on the history of
the country, starting, as far as Emma could tell, with the
Bronze Age. Marcy talked fast enough to cover the high
points in about two minutes, however, so Emma filled
her in on Italy Today and then taught her, with a tape re-
corder, to talk more and more slowly until she was almost coherent. When they were finally finished, she felt
that they both deserved an A.

Back in her apartment, she turned on a Sunday-night
news program and settled down to watch until she could
think of something she wanted to eat for dinner. Ab-

staining from Marcy's cookies, hot out of the oven, had been unlike her, and now her usual Sunday-night splurge, popcorn and ice cream, did not appeal. She considered heating up a can of soup, since the spring night was chilly enough for something warming, but that seemed like too much trouble, and she settled instead on grapes and cheese, because that was easy rather than because that was what she wanted. Emma loved food, loved to cook it and loved to eat it, and being able to serve herself whatever she wanted for dinner whenever she felt like eating it had been her first real pleasure after her divorce. And now she couldn't even enjoy that simple luxury. She was never a particularly moody person, and she was irritated with herself for being in such an all-pervasive funk. And then, on a sudden inspiration, she lifted Percy off her lap and went in to check the kitchen calendar and see when her period was due.

She was still leafing through the back months to see when she had last written it down—her celibate state made her much less anxious about keeping track—when the telephone rang and she jumped for it with a curious tightening of her stomach muscles.

"Hey, babe," she heard a familiar voice say.

"Tony," she answered, interpreting her let-down feeling as one of relief rather than disappointment. "You're not allowed to call me babe, remember?"

"Sorry, I forgot. So what have you been doing this weekend?"

"Never mind what I've been doing, what have *you* been doing? Who is she?"

"Who's who?"

"Who did you get all dolled up for last night?" she persisted, teasing. "New haircut, new suit."

"How did you know?" he yelled, instantly suspicious.

"Everybody knows. I announced it on the radio this morning."

"C'mon, Emma," he said, sounding wounded.

She relented. "George told me. He didn't really mean to tell me anything, he just said you were getting all dressed up and he assumed it was because of something you and I were doing."

"Oh." There was a silence. "How do you feel about that?"

"I think it's high time you had a haircut. You were looking like a real slob for a while there."

After another silence, Tony began again. "Emma, you're my good friend."

"I sure am, Tony."

"I think I found somebody I could be serious about."

"I wouldn't be a very good friend if I wasn't happy for you, would I?" she asked softly.

"You mean you don't mind?"

"Well, I hope it won't interfere with our friendship too much."

"I'm afraid she won't understand about us, though."

"Why don't you just tell her that I've always—" she began and then amended what she had been about to say. "Just explain that you've always felt like I was your sister. You've never felt anything more for me." That was not the exact truth, but it wouldn't do to remind Tony of some of the ups and downs their friendship had gone through in the past few years. For a while he had asked her to marry him, and when she had made it clear that she was not going to make any commitments, he had asked her to go to bed with him with no strings attached. Considering the confrontations they had had until he had accepted their relationship on her terms, it was a miracle they had any affection left for each other. If she was honest with herself, she had to admit that it was going to feel a little odd to have a constant source of admiration removed, but she was sincerely happy for him if he had found what he wanted.

"Well, yeah, maybe if I put it like that," he said, considering.

Emma could tell from his tone that this was too serious a matter to be teased about, so she stifled an inward sigh and prepared herself to listen to the whole, heart-warming story. "Tell me about her," she said encouragingly, and pulled up a chair for her feet so that she could stretch out and make herself comfortable.

"So for a faster wash and a brighter shine, take your car to Zippo's, where you'll get service with a smile or your money back." Emma let a modern rendition of "I Got It Bad and That Ain't Good" pick up speed on the turntable and leaned back in her chair with a sigh. She was having a terrible evening, and if she were Zippo, she would ask for her money back. Somehow she could not work up any enthusiasm for the newest car wash in town, and she was delivering everything from the weather report to the song introductions, when she could manage to think of something to say, in the same expressionless voice. It was her Thursday night jazz program, and Emma wasn't feeling very jazzy.

Playing nothing except torch songs didn't help, but it was hard to think of anything else to play. She toyed with the idea of playing only blues for the rest of the night, to insure that everybody else in town become as depressed as she was, but some largely repressed managerial instinct compelled her to turn around and search the shelves for something livelier. She had just put her finger on an instrumental recording by Dave Brubeck when the telephone rang. She answered it without giving herself time to wonder who it might be.

"Would you play 'I'm Getting Sentimental Over You' again? I won't be able to hear it, but at least one of us can."

"Simon?"

"Emma?" he parroted her.

"Hi." She sat and clutched the receiver, unsure what to say and feeling as if some fairy godmother had just waved a wand over her. After another scatterbrained moment, she mananged to pull her thoughts back to the business at hand. "Okay, but I can't play it every week. It's not my theme song."

"It is mine. Maybe you should save it for when I'm up there."

"Where are you?"

"New York. How was your week? And why on earth do you have an unlisted phone number?"

Emma felt that everything was moving a little too fast for her, and decided to concentrate on the simple question. "The police suggested it. I was having trouble with anonymous phone calls for a while."

"Yes, I suppose you would."

"They thought it was probably my ex-husband," she volunteered without quite knowing why.

"What a nasty fellow," he said mildly. "Can you meet me for a drink tomorrow night? I'll be getting in kind of late, but I thought if you were free around ten-thirty we could get together."

"Ten-thirty?" She pretended to consider it for a moment, pretended to be very casual. "Sure. Where do you want to meet?"

"How about the Inn again? It's a comfortable place to wait if I'm early, and if something should go wrong I can get a message to you."

"That's fine. I'll see you tomorrow, then."

"Good." He hesitated. "How was your week?"

"Oh, it was, uh...it was fine," she lied. "I had a good week."

"Hmmm. I had a lousy week." He hesitated again, and then said, "I'll look forward to seeing you tomorrow."

"Me, too," she said and hung up quickly. She hastily switched the sound to the other turntable, letting the Brubeck recording fill the studio with soft piano music, and sat back to consider. She could have sworn Simon was through with her, despite his professed desire to be friends. She had supposed that was simply a nice man's way of saying so long, but apparently when Simon Eliot said he would call, that's what he meant. She hoped he didn't want to give her any more lectures, not because she didn't feel she needed them, but because they made her so uncomfortable. How could you explain to a dynamic man like him that you were simply willing to settle for less? That life could move at a slower pace and still be full? She wondered if it was as simple as that, that he was a fast person and she was a slow person.

The reason she had been lying when she had told him she had had a good week was that she had spent the past five days wondering if she really was satisfied with her life in Litchfield. It was true that she felt safe in her little mountain community, and that feeling had been very important to her after her divorce. She had wanted everything to happen slowly, she had wanted life to be simple. But was that still enough? Should she bend to pressure and go back to New York, to more...action? For no matter how loving and supportive her family was, Emma herself often wondered if it really was all right to be in Litchfield.

Her little town had seemed rather dull lately, and she had finally realized it was because there wasn't anyone like Simon there. He would clearly never be satisfied there, and his presence in her life for two entire days was no more than a fluke. Even if he did buy property nearby, which she didn't think was likely once he'd had a good look around, he wouldn't really want to belong. He wouldn't be a part of her life. And she was beginning to think that perhaps she wanted someone like him in her life. She was careful to think of him as a type because thinking in specifics would get her nowhere.

She admired Simon, she decided as she thoughtlessly put on another record without bothering to see what it was. And at least she would not have to admire him from such a distance for a while. She could sit back and let him tell her stories from outside, as though he were some visitor from another planet and she were trapped on earth without her rocket ship. She smiled at the image and set about organizing her records, barely dismayed to find that she had been playing the latest hit single by Debby and the Deadbeats, "Kill."

Friday was brisk and cool and Emma decided to treat herself to her favorite activity. She dressed in jeans, sweater and a light jacket, picked up a map of the area and set off for the antique shops in the towns surrounding Litchfield. Part of the pleasure was simply in driving around the countryside and stumbling on little out-of-the-way shops, old homes nestled in the trees that she had never noticed before, little towns like Milton or Woodville or even New Preston, where she had gone with Simon. She rarely bought anything, because she did not have a lot of extra money and was trying to save enough for her own house one day. Besides, her apartment could not hold much more as it was. But she loved to look, loved to talk to the antique dealers, who would usually let her explore the contents of old trunks they had picked up at estate sales and not gone through yet, or let her go through their storage areas, looking for a little treasure under the piles of dusty, rotting furniture.

Emma had been a history major in college and she still felt a special reverence for American history, a feeling almost of nostalgia. She supposed that was why she loved old things, collected as much as she could and made a point of trying to discover the individual history of each piece. It was a way of being close to the past, and she felt much more comfortable thinking about the past than she did about the future.

She had been gone two hours, and was happily exploring the back room of a little shop in Bantam, when she first saw the pie safe. It was of oak, rather squat, and someone had partially removed a thick coating of pink paint from the wood. By some miracle, however, the tin sides were intact, with holes punched in a star pattern on both sides. She ran her hand over the smooth, exposed wood and looked wistfully for the price, knowing she wouldn't buy it no matter what it said. It was just the kind of piece she had a special weakness for, and she went in search of the dealer to learn where she had found it.

"That old safe? That's giving me such a headache. I mean, I've seen a lot of careless treatment of good furniture, but why anybody would paint an unoffending piece of oak pink is beyond me. I've got to spend another two days, at least, cleaning it up and I won't be able to charge enough to make it worth my while even then.

You can have it cheap if you want it." The woman glanced at her appraisingly over a pair of half glasses that were perched on her nose and secured by a long black ribbon. They had done a little business together before—Emma had bought a quilt and a couple of dishes from her—but she wasn't one of her regular stops, and she wondered exactly what she meant by "cheap."

"Where did you get it?"

"It was part of an estate sale. Whole house full of furniture that had been in the family for years, and when the old lady died they just sold everything. I think they live in New York now and they just didn't need it, but you wouldn't think they would practically give it away like that."

Emma went back to admire the safe again. It was shorter and narrower than most she had seen. On the inside it had two oak shelves, which had been covered in contact paper that would peel off easily enough. It would be perfect to hold her linens. It would be perfect in the hall just outside her bedroom door. She could put a little antique fruit bowl on it that she had bought impulsively without having a good place to display it.

She tried to think of a good reason why she should not buy it, but there simply weren't any. When she had been in college, she had been planning to write her thesis on early-American women, and had hoped at the time to go on and get her Ph.D. and specialize in the subject. She had always been amazed at the curiously blank spot in American history when it came to the subject of women, as though no one had bothered to record their presence. Private journals and letters were rare, and most research had to be done simply by looking at the things they left behind, quilts, paintings, hand-painted dishes. With a few bits of scattered evidence it was possible to decipher an outline, but never a complete picture, of what their lives had been like. It was an inadequate basis for a dissertation, but Emma was just fantasizing now and it was all right to draw a few conclusions from insufficient evidence.

She wanted the pie safe for her own whimsical reasons, but she knew that once some other woman had wanted it for purely practical reasons, had coaxed her husband or brother to build it for her, had had the tin shipped in and hammered out, perhaps by the blacksmith, had traded some livestock or perhaps some handmade articles of her own in order to pay for it. Emma was fighting a losing battle. The longer she stared at it, the more she wanted it. She went back to the front of the store to find the proprietor, now sorting through a chest of old silver. "Do you take checks?" she asked, with a curiously resigned sigh.

Five

When Emma finally pulled up in front of the Lyon's Inn Friday night, it was already just past ten-thirty and she hadn't stopped moving all day. She had tied the safe in the trunk of her little car and hurried home from Bantam, eager to get started on stripping the paint. The safe was now sitting on several layers of newspaper in the middle of the kitchen, surrounded by pots of caustic paint remover and sticky balls of steel wool, and despite the open windows and the fact that she had had a shower, Emma felt as though she could still smell the chemicals she had been immersed in all afternoon. Her hands were stained brown and slightly burnt, but she didn't mind. She had succeeded in scraping off most of the top layer of paint, and she could tell the little safe was going to be beautiful.

She parked the car and entered the lobby, glancing around for Simon as she approached the desk and half expecting to see him stretched out in the same chair she had found him in the previous week. There was a small group of business people standing around the fireplace, following some unconscious heat-seeking instinct since there was no fire, and although she glanced over them hopefully, he wasn't among them. She approached the same sleepy desk clerk and learned that Simon had not checked in yet, and no, there was no message for her.

Emma turned away uncertainly, not wanting to hang around and wait for him too long, and not wanting to miss him either. She wandered over closer to the bar to escape the uninquisitive but still irritating eyes of the desk clerk, and was just making up her mind to leave when there was a slight commotion by the door and Simon burst in, "burst" because he filled the door frame with himself and his bags, and because the atmosphere in the room underwent a subtle change when he entered. It wasn't that his presence was particularly commanding, but he gave the room a certain focus it had lacked before and carried in a gust of excitement that sent a rush through Emma's veins. She stood a good twenty paces away, but her body shuddered lightly as though she felt a draft from the open door. She started to glance around the room to see how the other occupants were reacting to his entrance, but he spotted her and she forgot everything else, never realizing that no one else in the room had seen fit to do more than glance up briefly.

"I'm late," he said, crossing over to her immediately. "I had a flat tire about twenty miles down the road and I decided after I fixed it that I could be here in less time than it took to find a phone. They close the desk in fifteen minutes, so let me just check in and take these things to my room and get cleaned up."

Emma blinked up at him as he stood over her with a suitcase in one hand and a briefcase in the other, his dark hair tousled and his hands grimy, mute evidence of the flat tire. He made her feel as if she were standing in a strong wind, and she wasn't quite sure she liked it. "Okay," she said faintly and followed in his wake over to the desk, where he completed checking in, unmindful of the clerk's distasteful look at his hands. He turned and motioned for her to precede him up the stairs to his room, and then ushered her through the door with something akin to pride.

"I reserved the same room I had last weekend. Isn't this nice?"

"It's lovely," she said, walking in and instantly coveting a washstand, complete with basin and pitcher. It wasn't a large room, but the window formed one of the gables on the third floor overlooking the front yard, and contained a charming little window seat with crewel-work pillows. The furniture was all oak, simple and sturdy, and it looked as though nothing had been changed for two hundred years, with the exception of the discreet wiring of the lamps and a tiny little bathroom right inside the door, as though the twentieth century would be catered to, but only just.

Simon disappeared into the bathroom and she could hear vigorous splashing—did he do everything vigorously?—as she wandered aimlessly about the room, fingering the quilt on the bed, running a hand along the dresser, turning over the water pitcher to see if it had any distinguishing marks. After a minute she heard through the door "So what have you been up to lately?"

"Antiquing," she answered, absently fingering the dresser scarf.

"Looking for anything in particular?" he asked, coming out of the bathroom as he finished drying off his face.

"Not really, I just like to look, but I found this great oak pie safe. It was covered with several different coats of paint, and the woman practically gave it to me so she wouldn't have to strip it herself, but I can tell it's going to be really beautiful."

"What, exactly, is a pie safe?" he asked, leaning against the wall and studying her with a slight look of amusement on his face.

"Well, it's a place where you keep pies," she answered, launching into the explanation. "Or food of any type. The real ones have perforated tin on the sides, and a lot of times people removed that and replaced it with wood or painted over it. The great thing about this one is that the original tin is still there and it looks pretty good. What I thought I'd do—" she said and then caught sight of the look on his face, the slight twist at the side of his lips. He didn't know what a pie safe was and he didn't really care. They had so little in common. She needed to remember that he was more or less from another planet; he was a hotshot New York television producer and had a different system of values. "I thought I'd just fix it up and use it," she finished lamely.

Emma was correct in thinking Simon wasn't drinking in the details concerning the pie safe but incorrect in thinking he didn't really care. He had come back to Litchfield because he had found it next to impossible to stay away, and he had decided the simplest thing would be to see Emma again and figure out why she was irresistible to him. He had also taken the time to actually make an appointment with a real estate agent without bothering to seriously analyze his motives. He thought perhaps Emma might get around to asking why he'd come, and he didn't want her to think he had come up just to see her, which of course he had.

Her manner toward him was a little less hesitant than it had been the weekend before, and he found that encouraging. She seemed more relaxed, as well, but he put that down to possible fatigue.

She was standing by the small lamp on the dresser opposite the bed, and while her eyes were shadowed, he thought he could detect a sign of strain around her mouth. The light was casting auburn highlights in her abundant hair and she seemed, for a moment, to be lit up somehow from within. "Ready for that drink now?" he asked, more to fill the sudden silence between them than because he really wanted to drink.

"All right."

He made no effort to move away from the wall. "It's good to see you again," he said softly.

"It's good to see you, too," she answered, and smiled. Emma had not intended for the smile to be voluptuous or suggestive in any way. It had begun with a slight widening of her long green eyes, a sudden unavoidable light leaping up in them that was quickly veiled by her thick lashes, which dropped heavily down again almost as quickly as they had risen. Her mouth remained slightly open, her lips curving up, and the lower half of her face was somehow more relaxed, as though she had been waiting for him to say that and was relieved now that he finally had.

It all happened in less than a breath and left Simon wondering why he hadn't tried to find an opportunity to kiss her when he first saw her. He hadn't given himself time; he hadn't been sure he wanted to, but he was sure now and he wondered if it was too late. He took his hand off the doorknob and took a step toward her, and she didn't move away or even look alarmed. Her lips were still slightly parted, her eyes fastened on his face now, and when he took another step and caught her shoulders, pulling her to him, she tilted her face up and closed her eyes, waiting for him to kiss her. Simon stared down at her for another moment, wondering what gods were smiling on him now, before bending down and angling his head slightly to touch her lips with his.

The first sensation Emma was aware of was an approaching source of heat, and when her lips were brushed with a quick, gentle kiss she felt a brief shiver of disappointment. She had wanted more. In the next second, however, Simon's grip on her shoulders tightened and his lips came down on hers again, firmer but still gentle, lingering and rubbing over hers with sheer tactile pleasure. She felt herself being drugged by the sensation, dependent on his nearness and his warmth, and when his hot tongue slipped between her lips she felt a wave of shock and delight rush through her body. She wrapped her arms around his waist in order to tether herself to something solid, bringing their bodies together and feeling the unmistakable hardness of his need. His hands ran down her back and pressed her firmly against him, and a ripple of hot sensation that had been coursing through her veins was suddenly centered in her lower body, where she felt the answering pulse in his.

Emma had temporarily lost her mind, lost it to the dominant forces of need and want, and when she felt Simon propelling her carefully backward she aquiesced, letting him guide her onto the bed and fall heavily on top of her. He pinned her arms over her head with one hand, running the other possessively over her breasts and belly while his tongue pressed hers with a new insistence. She felt her own body loosening and softening in response, felt herself opening wider, and she moaned softly, inciting him to drive himself into her despite the frustrating barriers of clothing.

With a sound that was something like a snarl he tore off his loosened tie and raised himself up enough to shrug off his jacket and shirt. He then quickly turned his attention to Emma, helping her out of the blouse she had already unbuttoned, unhooking her bra and tossing it aside. In a breathless voice she whispered, "Simon, please," and he mistook it for a protest when it was a plea in earnest.

"Just let me look at you," he whispered, cradling her nakedness in his arms and delighting her aroused nipples with the bristling curls on his chest.

Clumsy with haste and frustration, she reached down to unfasten his belt. He had to make love to her—she would die if he didn't. He embodied some vital force that was necessary for her survival, and she began fumbling with the button on her skirt.

"Emma, I don't want to rush you," he whispered, raising his teasing lips from her nipple and looking down at her with blue eyes that were almost black with desire. Unable to think of the right thing to say, she shook her head and wrapped her leg around one of his, arching herself into him and pulling his head back down to her breast.

Her skirt was quickly removed and she breathed a sigh of relief when she finally felt his naked length on hers, his arousal pressing knowingly into her taut belly. "Now," she whispered, curving her arms around him and pulling him against her. He tantalized her with his lips and hands, hesitating until she thought she couldn't bear the pleasure he aroused, before he slipped between her thighs and guided himself into her welcoming depths.

She gasped at the unaccustomed sensation, but then pleasure took over once again. He had paused while her body adapted to his, but when he could tell she was ready, he began thrusting in long, hard strokes, pushing her onto another plane of feeling. Emma had never known a man could feel like that, had never been moved to such a heady feeling of enjoyment so intense it was close to intolerable.

Simon's face was pressed into the side of hers, one hand still caressing her breast while he became lost in the sweet fire of her body. She looked wildly beautiful as she was carried away by passion, her big eyes luminous and an excitement in her expression that replaced her customary look of wary stillness. He had found a core of life and energy she had been repressing for too long, and he plunged in victoriously, coaxing her response, drawing it out as a series of shudders gripped her and pulled him deeper inside. He finally had to give in to his own unbearable passion, thrusting convulsively, dimly aware of her urgent hands on his hips.

For a long moment afterward they lay together in exhausted silence, Simon planting an occasional kiss on her damp skin while Emma felt as though she were returning to consciousness after a wild dream. She couldn't believe she had actually made love to this man. She barely knew him, wasn't sure what she wanted from him, could barely remember how it had all come about. One moment they were chatting about her pie safe, perfectly chummy, and then everything had changed with a look.

She still liked the feel of him on top of her and the fact that he was tenderly kissing the curve of her jaw, so when he pulled away, she felt momentarily bereft. ''I didn't expect this to happen, or I would have been prepared," he said apologetically.

He was clearly missing the significance of what had happened. "I know you didn't," she began in a choked voice. "You just wanted to be my friend."

He silenced her with a finger on her lips. "No, I wanted to be your lover. I just thought you'd put up more of a struggle."

At that she started to rise, needing to be alone to sort things out. "I should leave," she said, but he stopped her again.

"No, you shouldn't. Just sleep with me tonight. I know you've got a lot of questions, but nothing is going to change overnight, and you'll be able to think more clearly in the morning." He was holding her to the bed with one arm, as though he refused to let her leave, or even get up, but his expression was mild and earnest, and Emma knew if she said one word of protest he would let her go without a fight. It was easier not to say anything, however, so she gave in and curled up next to him, falling innocently asleep.

Emma's normal waking process was long, involved and luxurious. It began with a return of bodily awareness, a consciousness of the fact that she was in a soft, warm bed with her eyes closed and her limbs heavily relaxed. She usually took a moment to stretch, to make the most of this state that was both vulnerable and warmly secure, before opening her eyes to take stock of the quality of light that filled her bedroom, to run her eyes over the familiar furnishings that filled her needs so exactly. Emma believed her bedroom was the most perfect place in the world, a veritable pleasure to wake up in, and it was something more than a brutal shock to open her eyes and have them alight on a strange, if perfectly charming, window seat. She was next able to identify a slight physical discomfort as a draft around her upper regions, and she turned her head slowly, her sleepy mind relying only on sensory perception to interpret this unfamiliar state.

The next moment brought a wealth of information and recollection. There was a man lying on his side next to her, his head propped up on one hand, his eyes fully awake if slightly droopy, his gaze resting on her bare breasts. It was Simon. Emma remembered everything about the previous evening, and she still could not prevent a blush as she moved to pull the sheet up over her chest. His hand stopped her. "What are you doing?" she asked, her voice still sleepy and confused.

"Watching you."

"Why? What am I doing?"

"You've been trying to wake up. I'm not sure you've succeeded yet."

"Sorry. It takes me a while."

"Don't apologize. I've enjoyed it." Emma blushed again and pulled the sheet up over her breasts, but he pulled it back down to her waist again. "Just lie there and let me admire you." He raised his hand as if to touch her and then let it fall again. "You know, before I came up last weekend a friend of mine told me I'd find a little wood nymph waiting for me here in the trees."

Emma started to squirm. "For one thing, you 'found' me at the radio station, and for another thing, I'm not particularly nymphlike."

"Are you kidding? You're perfect," he said in a teasing voice. "My very own Daphne."

"Yes, and we both know what happened to her," she scoffed. "I always thought that was a rotten thing for her father to do."

"You don't think she was better off being turned into a laurel tree than suffering Apollo's advances?"

"Well, I always thought she probably regretted it later."

"Yes, she probably did," he said. "You and Daphne have more than one thing in common, you know."

She felt a quick flush rising, thinking he was referring to her own tendency to run when things got complicated, to turn down what looked like golden opportunities. "Don't scold me now," she said with an attempt at being lighthearted. "It's too early in the morning."

"I wasn't going to scold," he said, running his finger between her rosy breasts. "I was referring to your physical attributes, your, um, classical perfection." She lay perfectly still while his finger outlined her body, tracing the gentle slope of her belly, the curving lines under her breasts, the smooth junction of neck and shoulder.

When Simon was fifteen he had visited, with his parents, a small museum in Athens that was not well supplied with guards. Finding himself alone in a room with a marble statue, a young woman carrying a water jug on her head, he had not been able to resist running his hand over the smooth lines, softened by age. It wasn't the prurient curiosity of a young boy that had compelled him to do it; it was the undeniable instinct of a sensuous man, and the memory had resided in his palm until now. The woman beneath him was almost as still, as completely available, as her marble predecessor, but the warmth of her flesh and the darkening and tightening of her nipple when he touched it with his fingertip were unforgettable reminders of her humanity.

He felt drawn to her warmth, moving to slide his skin over hers, and his mind made another leap, and he found himself thinking of a Renoir painting of a naked woman bathing. The background of the painting was filled with a hazy, golden light and the water was just visible glistening on her shoulders. Her skin looked as cool to the touch as Emma's had been that day she had fallen in the lake, and moved by the memory, he ran his tongue up her neck to her ear. Her eyes were closed and she was breathing rapidly, and her body smelled a little like perfume and a little like love.

Suddenly needing to know more of her, Simon moved down her body to the steamy center of her femininity, running his tongue along her inner thigh, burying his face in her damp, perfumy flesh and bringing her to a delicious tension with his exploring tongue. Her body instantly arched and shuddered, and he rose back up and entered her still quivering flesh with his own hungry arousal. After only a few long strokes he pulled away from her, moving to lie beside her and support himself on one arm. He loved the quick look of dismay that flashed across her face when he had withdrawn. "Emma," he whispered, reaching to take her hand in his and drawing it down. "Touch me." He released her fingers when they came in contact with his hardened shaft, moving his flesh along her waiting hand, which finally curved in response.

She watched his face as she learned the contours of his flesh, being guided by his response, the flicker of his dark lashes where they rested on his pale skin, the quickly indrawn breath as he pushed her hand away. She reached out for him again, loving to please him, but he was too quick, entering her with one long push. She let him take over, devouring her neck with his teeth, plundering her mouth with his own, moaning an incoherent message close to her ear. She had not expected to be aroused again so quickly, but his body worked a magic on hers she had never known before, and she gave in to the feeling, reaching a peak and clinging to him blindly while his own wild plunging brought him to a climax.

Simon seemed to fall asleep on top of her after that, and Emma was grateful for the chance to be alone with her thoughts, if only for a moment or two. They had slipped back into it so easily, slipped back into easy talk, making love like longtime lovers. He had caught her when her defenses were down, still vulnerable from sleep, and she wondered if he had done it deliberately or if he had just been letting it happen, as she had been.

She certainly had been aggressive the night before, she thought, and she cringed slightly at the memory of how she had pulled impatiently at his clothes, demanding he make love to her even before they were both ready. She was not used to wanting a man so badly, or to admitting she really wanted one at all. Ralph had considered himself a good lover; he had taken care to point out his skill to her, and he was perfectly all right. But with Simon there was a chemistry that clamored to be recognized, and she found that refusing to act on it was impossible. Moreover, it seemed like the right thing to do. Emma did not have a strict moral code, preferring to stumble along doing what seemed at the time to be the right thing to do and not always bothering to analyze the hows and whys. And making love to Simon simply felt right. Their bodies fit, even though he was so much bigger. His hands knew just where to touch her without her having to instruct him, and hers apparently did the same thing for him.

She did feel a little embarrassed about the fact that as soon as they were in a bedroom together they had fallen into bed. And while it hadn't happened when he had come to her room last weekend, that was thanks only to his self-control, not hers. But Emma thought about it for a while and decided to do something uncharacteristic—she decided to take what was offered instead of saying no. She had been saying no more and more often in the past few years, and she suspected that wasn't good for her. She wanted to have an affair with Simon, and she was going to do something to promote it. She wondered how serious he was about looking at property in the area.

She shifted slightly beneath his weight and moved her shoulder away from his prickly chin. He was sound asleep now, breathing heavily on her neck, and she felt a little like a squashed ant, but she didn't mind. She thought that the next step would be to cook dinner for him—after all, she owed him dinner and he had already taken her to the one really nice restaurant in Litchfield. The only way to serve a comparable dinner was to fix it herself. Emma was an excellent cook, but her urge to cook dinner for a man was wrapped up in an urge to take care of him, and she had a corresponding urge to avoid getting in that position again with anybody. She also had a private theory that men think less of women who try to take care of them, and that serving Simon dinner would be demeaning in some way. She didn't see any easy way out of the problem and was relieved when Simon stirred, muttered something against her skin that provoked a brief shiver of goose bumps down her arms and rather abruptly woke up. He raised his head and looked at her with wide eyes, eyes that had a curious trick of appearing to be innocent, and then, just as she had done, suddenly recollected who she was and where he was.

"How long have I been crushing you?" he asked.

"Not long."

He rolled off her and sat up in the bed, and she pulled herself up to sit beside him, not bothering to try to cover herself with the sheet this time. "Good grief, it's almost ten o'clock," he exclaimed, putting his watch back on the night table. "I've got to get moving." He took her hand and pulled her off the bed after him, asking, "Want to take a shower?" and taking her affirmative answer for granted. The shower was just barely big enough for the two of them, and Simon soaped her as industriously as he had soaped himself, apparently believing that another way to stay clean was simply to intimidate the dirt. If she hadn't known for a fact that his touch could be so gentle, she would never have believed it.

"I'll do my own hair," she said, putting out a hand to stop him from pouring a large amount of shampoo on her head.

"You don't like to have somebody else wash your hair?" he asked, surprised.

"I love it. I'm just afraid I won't have any left if I let you."

He grinned. "Sorry. I'm in a hurry." He went to work on his own head and they stood in the tub, facing each other below their respective crowns of lather, pleased with themselves and almost childlike. "So what are you going to do today?"

"I think I'll finish up the pie safe. The station's covered for the day."

"Mm-hm. Want to meet me for dinner?"

"Why don't you let me cook for you?" she asked, glad he had made it so easy for her.

"That would be fine, if you like to cook," he replied, tilting his head back under the water to rinse.

Emma thought she detected something in his tone that she wasn't sure about. "I do like to cook. What's wrong with that?" she asked defensively.

"Nothing," he said, moving out of the water and letting her step into it. "I'm just not a very good cook myself."

"I cook very well. Do you have a thing against women who cook, or something?" she asked, sputtering under the water and half-aware that she was being ridiculous, but determined to get to the bottom of this anyway.

"Emma, for heaven's sake!" he exclaimed, deciding she had rinsed well enough and reaching behind her to turn off the water. "If you like to cook, cook. It's not that complicated."

"It is, too. My ex-husband always made a big deal about trying to get me to food him," she muttered.

Simon tossed a towel around her neck and used it as a lasso to haul her up to his chest, looking down into her upturned face. "Stop judging half of the human race on the basis of one stupid jerk, okay?"

"Okay," she said in a small voice.

He kissed her firmly on the mouth, still holding her wet body next to his with the towel, and then kissed her five more times in rapid succession. "Did anyone ever tell you you're a pain in the ass?"

"I—I don't think so."

"Hmm. Figures." He pulled the towel over her face, giving her hair a brisk rub, and then turned away to dry himself. "What kind of wine do you want me to bring?"

"Red," she said, still feeling a little uncertain about their exchange.

"And what time should I come?"

"I don't know. Around seven-thirty or eight, I suppose." She followed him into the bedroom, padding naked around the room collecting her clothes from the previous night while he dressed in a crisp shirt and tie and the business suit that was crumpled on the floor. She finally approached him, wearing only her bra and panties, and said, "Am I really a pain in the ass?"

He was sitting on the side of the bed, pulling on his socks, but he stopped and looked up at her, amusement belying the look of concern in his eyes. "That bothered you, didn't it?" he asked. "Everybody worth knowing is a pain in the ass sometimes, Emma. It means you have a personality."

"Oh, so that was a compliment. I see," she said, nodding her head wisely.

"Exactly," he said, returning his attention to his socks, an irrepressible grin forming around his mouth.

Emma studied him for another minute, deciding what form her revenge should take, before snatching his sock back off his foot and tackling him, throwing her weight against him and making him fall back onto the bed. "Pain in the ass, huh? I'll give *you* a pain in the ass." She pulled his shirt out of his pants sufficiently to stick her hand in at the side and tickle him, delighting in watching him writhe convulsively only until he had gathered his strength enough to toss her off and pin her to the bed.

"See what I mean?" he asked, glaring down at her with a gleam in his eyes. "You're just proving my point."

"But now I have a weapon against you, so you'd better watch your step."

"So had you. I tend to throw up after being tickled violently."

"Do you really?" she asked, wide-eyed.

"Yes, I really do." He nodded twice and then added, "But you're safe enough for now." He continued looking down at her, the look on his face and the meaning of his words changing subtly. "Unfortunately." He still did not get up.

"You're all mussed up, Simon," she said softly. "You can't go out like that." The moment passed, and by the time he had stood up and straightened his clothes and combed his hair, she was dressed as well.

"I'll see you tonight, then," he said, standing by the door.

"Okay." She watched him leave, and then turned back to the mirror to start combing out her tangled hair. Her cheeks were slightly pink and her eyes had a soft look in them that she had never noticed before, and she stopped what she was doing and studied herself for a moment. She was fully aware of the fact that she was doing something rash as far as her emotions were concerned. A woman like her could not become sexually involved with a man and not be emotionally involved as well, and she would simply have to trust both her own instincts, and Simon. That was a demand she had not made of herself in a long time.

She turned away from the mirror and located her purse and shoes. She had a lot to do today if she wanted to finish the safe and clear out her kitchen so that she could cook in it. She wanted everything to be perfect despite her resolution that this meal not "mean" anything, and she wanted to make her plans and then get to the market as early as possible so that she would have the best meats and vegetables available. She also wanted to be well out of Simon's room before the maid came along. She gathered her things, glanced hastily around, and slipped out into the quiet hallway.

Six

———

Tenderloin, eh? Anybody I know?'' Emma started and turned to find Stu standing next to her, surveying her from beneath impossibly arched eyebrows. When she flushed guiltily, Stu batted her lashes flirtatiously. "Oh, Emma, you don't have to serve me tenderloin just because we've been friends for so long. A good steak will do, honest.''

"Hi." Emma gulped and tried to look nonchalant while the butcher weighed the meat she had indicated, and then she uttered a despairing little cry when he informed her of the price.

"It's a good one, Emma. It'll melt in your mouth," the butcher promised and then added, "And it's good for you, too, honey." He had a slight crush on Emma, but not enough to be unhappy that she was buying beef tenderloin for another man. And Emma, knowing the wisdom of not alienating one's butcher, smiled appreciatively and handed over the requisite money without any more fuss. She waited while Stu bought a pound of ground beef and then left the store with her, walking leisurely along Main Street with her purchases slung over her shoulder in a string bag.

"I take it Boy Wonder is back in town?" Stu began once they were clear of possible eavesdroppers.

"He sure is."

"I knew all he wanted was dinner."

"It was my idea," Emma reprimanded. "And besides, I owe him dinner and it's cheaper to cook it than it is to buy it."

"Mm-hm. And you know what's going to happen when you spend all that time alone together in your apartment," Stu reminded her. From her tone of voice it was impossible to believe that the two women were the same age.

"My apartment smells like paint remover, which isn't very suggestive. And besides," she added in a rare, confessional spirit, "it's a little late to worry about that."

Emma had attempted to speak nonchalantly, but her statement still stopped Stu in her tracks. "Good grief! That's not like you."

"Well, I didn't mean to," she explained. "It just happened."

"Honey, I think it's great!" Stu reassured her. "You just got carried away, didn't you? It's about time." She paused to consider the situation, and then added, "You must really like this one, huh?"

"Yes," Emma admitted in a small voice.

"Can I come dance at your wedding?"

"I wouldn't start limbering up just yet. I told you if I ever acted as if I wanted to get married again, to have me committed."

"Oh, Emma, stop being so cynical. Marriage is the happiest state to live in that I know."

"You were lucky," she reminded her softly. "I wasn't. And I'm not going to try my luck again anytime soon." She changed her tone to a teasing one. "Besides, don't you think I'm making great strides? At least I'm having an affair."

"That's better than nothing," Stu agreed. "Fill me in on the details when he leaves. I have to run."

Emma made her way back to her apartment feeling relaxed and curiously confident. While she was a popular figure in town, she was also, due to her position, a powerful figure, and she never was entirely sure she was liked for herself. She had no doubts about Stu's friendship, of course. Stu had come upon her the day after she had moved to Litchfield, right after she had dropped two full grocery bags onto the sidewalk in front of her building. She had had a hard two days, moving on adrenaline alone long after her ordinary strength had been exhausted, and she supposed that her arms had simply carried too many heavy boxes and pieces of furniture. They gave out when she was halfway to the front door, and the bags landed with an ominously solid thud on the concrete. Emma had looked down at the mess at her feet for a moment and then simply sat down, temporarily overcome by the enormity of rolling cans of cat food, a broken jar of mayonnaise and the dreadful whooshing sound of kitty litter running out unchecked onto the sidewalk.

Stu confessed later that her first thought had been that Emma was having a heart attack and she was hoping for a chance to try out the CPR she had just been taught. While she was mildly disappointed to find Emma perfectly healthy, she had still been nice about helping her clean up the mess. Emma, in turn, had been nice about letting Marcy, who was still a toddler, play with the eight-week-old Percy, purchased two days earlier in a fit of loneliness.

After their initial meeting they discovered they were nearly neighbors, and when Emma began frequenting the Towne Restaurant they had gradually become absorbed into each other's lives. Stu was a sincere friend and she made Emma feel good. But Simon's unconcealed pleasure with her, his obvious admiration and enjoyment of her, made her feel curiously renewed. She moved with a newfound grace she was barely conscious of.

When she got home she started marinating the tenderloin in wine and herbs, and then mixed together the ingredients for a small, densely chocolate cake. She didn't know just how Simon felt about dessert, but she herself felt that dinner wasn't dinner unless it ended with something sweet. That was one of her vices, but she felt disposed to forgive herself today. She waited until the cake was baked and chilling in the refrigerator before going to work on the pie safe, so that the smelly fumes would not color the taste of everything in the kitchen. She removed the rest of the paint easily, dried off the wood, moved the stripped safe back into the hall and, by opening all the windows and running the fan until she was shivering, managed to clear the apartment of the smell.

By the time she was finished it was after six, and still early enough in the season to be getting dark and chilly. She showered, decided to dress simply in slacks and a pretty new sweater, and then tied an apron around herself and began chopping fresh vegetables for a mixed sauté. She was just finishing the mushrooms when the doorbell rang and she went to let Simon in.

"I'm early," he said, handing her a bottle of red wine and a bunch of flowers done up in green tissue paper.

"That's okay," she said, lifting up the top fold of paper to find a bunch of purple, white and yellow irises. "Oh, aren't they beautiful! Thank you, Simon." She stood on tiptoe and lightly kissed his lips.

"Thank *you*," he said, catching her around the waist with one arm and returning the kiss, quite a bit more firmly and soulfully than Emma had. "You're awfully nice to find at the end of the day," he said when he had straightened up and stood looking down at her, holding her against him.

Emma's heart gave a queer little turn and she pulled away gently, saying, "I have to put these in water." He didn't really mean anything by what he said, she knew, but he had said it, and she didn't know what the proper response was.

Simon removed his jacket and tie and followed her into the kitchen, where she stood arranging the flowers in a glass vase. He came up behind her and held her, resting his chin on her shoulder and reaching a long arm around to adjust a tall, yellow iris that she had put in the center of the arrangement. "I'm not in your way, am I?" he asked, taking another flower away from her and putting it where he thought it ought to go.

Emma eyed him out of the corner of her long, green eye. "If you're not careful I'm going to make you set the table, or something."

"I'll set the table," he said, straightening up.

"No, you won't do it right. Why don't you fix yourself a drink and relax?"

"I'm too keyed up to relax," he said, pacing the kitchen behind her. "Oh, I almost forgot to tell you the good news, or good news for me, anyway. My office called to tell me they've tracked down a Germaine Marque in Paris who's an old friend of Edmonds's, a contemporary. I guess they must have been lovers. Anyway, now she's what we call an "eccentric," but I may be able to sweet-talk her into introducing him at the dinner."

Emma had finished with the flowers and had returned to her vegetables, and at Simon's announcement a still, tight feeling gripped her stomach, and she quietly laid the knife aside rather than cut off her thumb with it. Simon had found her Scotch and was busy mixing it with soda, and failed to notice her reaction. She concentrated very hard on a small pile of snow peas while she tried to assimilate what was happening.

Despite the finality with which she had turned down his second request for her to speak, she had begun to wonder lately if she had made the right decision. She hadn't had any really serious doubts, but she had enjoyed mulling over the possibility of maybe, if coaxed, changing her mind. How dare he take her at her word so completely? How could he expect her to make such an important decision in so little time? She had half anticipated being sweet-talked, as he put it, into agreeing with his proposition. She had rehearsed her arguments in her mind, explaining her excellent reasons for refusing, seeing him dejected yet beginning to accept, eventually, her decision. And here he had gone and dropped her entirely without, apparently, much regret. She supposed people who were qualified to introduce Willis Edmonds at a testimonial dinner were, to Simon, a dime a dozen.

She realized she was being ridiculous and was disgusted with herself for it, disgusted as she surveyed the pile of neatly chopped vegetables on the counter. She was mad at both of them. Was she merely toying with him? No. More importantly, was he toying with her? Would he want to keep seeing her, now that he was no longer interested in getting her to speak? She decided to delicately probe his motives. "So how was your day with the real estate agent?" she asked unconcernedly.

"I didn't spend much time with her," he answered nonchalantly. "I don't know how serious I am about investing in property right now."

And that settles that, she thought as she began furiously stringing the peas. "Not serious about much, are you?" she muttered sotto voce.

"What did you say?"

"Nothing," she answered, tossing a broccoli she had lost patience with back into the refrigerator. When she looked up he was watching her with a puzzled look on his face, and she gave him a quick, artificial smile before turning away.

Dinner was not a success. The salad dressing had too much vinegar in it, but Emma decided it suited her disposition perfectly and she left it the way it was. The tenderloin was overcooked, and she had thrown all the chopped vegetables into the frying pan at once, with the result that the mushrooms were cooked until they completely lost their character and the carrots were unpleasantly crunchy. The conversation was no more inspiring. Simon continued to regard her with a mystified look in his baby-blue eyes, trusting eyes, she decided, but perhaps not trustworthy. He tried to question her about her day but she would not cooperate, carefully monitoring her monosyllabic answers so that he would not be able to object outright to anything she said, or to challenge her about whether there was something wrong. Noncommunication was an art, and Emma was good at it.

Simon finally gave up and started telling her about his upcoming trip to France. He was planning to go over with the director of the documentary and then hopefully turn the entire project over to him. Jack Morissey. An excellent director. He liked Paris, he told her; hadn't been for several months and was looking forward to being there in the spring.

Emma thought that was just great. She hoped he would have a wonderful time. Would he like a piece of chocolate cake with his coffee?

Even the cake was too sweet. She took one bite and pushed her plate away, and noted that Simon's expression was relieved as he saw her plate, and he left more than half of his own piece untouched.

It was finally over. She stood up from the table and started collecting the dirty dishes. "If you'll excuse me while I clean up," she mumbled, hoping that he would get bored enough to leave. She filled the sink with hot, sudsy water and began scrubbing each dish furiously, as though they were all contaminated with something deadly and it was up to her to sanitize them. Simon did not join her, and she supposed he was still sitting at the table with the same grim look on his face that she had left him with.

She felt a momentary twinge as she thought about how mean she was being, but she resolutely quashed it. She was sorry she got involved with him, even sorrier she had made love to him twice already. That only made him that much harder to get over, and she suspected that the next man to come along, if there ever was one, would be dull and stupid by comparison. But there was a certain safety in dull, stupid men, she reminded herself. She wondered briefly if Simon had lost interest in her before yesterday, but she didn't think that was being entirely fair. The episode in his hotel room last night had obviously taken him as much by surprise as it had her, unless he had made the trip to Connecticut solely for the purpose of seducing her, which she didn't think was very likely. He didn't seem to be the devious type, she thought with a sigh as she began scrubbing the roaster, but perhaps he was flighty. He had told her once that he was afraid he would not have time to do all he wanted to do in this life, and perhaps that included knowing as many women as possible. She should have been warned.

By the time she was rinsing the last dish, Emma was beginning to feel guilty. She even felt a little sorry for Simon. Poor boy probably thought she was his type, and was out simply for a good time. She couldn't imagine how they had managed to misjudge each other, and supposed they both simply had seen what they had wanted to see. She set the pan in the drainboard and hastily sponged down the counter, not bothering to tidy up as well as usual. It was time to face the music, or whatever it was that was awaiting her.

Simon was, in fact, sitting just as she had left him, as though she had only stepped out of the room for one minute instead of twenty. He glanced up when she came in, a waiting, watchful look on his face as though he didn't quite trust her and wanted to see what she would do next. She was no longer a known quantity.

Emma felt a passing sense of power that was quickly replaced by dread of what was to come. Her stomach suddenly knotted itself in the same coil she used to feel when her father was about to scold her and for a moment she hated both men for their ability to intimidate her.

The nervous anticipation increased when Simon stood up and moved over to the couch, carefully pushing the coffee table out of range before he sat. "Come here," he ordered, patting the place beside him.

She silently obeyed, noting that his expression was now one of forced casualness. She didn't have to cooperate, she told herself obstinately, and stiffened when he laid an arm around her shoulders.

"Are you sure there isn't something bothering you?" he asked, giving her one last chance to be reasonable and adult.

"Positive," she answered lightly.

"Good." He leaned closer, running a finger down her cheek with the hand that had been resting on her shoulder, lightly tickling the down on her skin. Emma wanted to turn to him, to hide from his exploring hand in the warmth of his body, but she willed herself not to move, not to respond.

"I thought you were acting as if you were angry for some reason," Simon continued, his lips alarmingly close to her ear, close enough that she could feel his hot breath fanning the sensitive skin of her neck. "I wondered if you had something against irises."

Emma knew she wasn't going to be let off easy. Simon was now delicately fingering her curls, pulling slightly, sensuously, twining them around his fingers to admire their silky texture. She would have to say or do something to distract him, because her own body was ready to betray her. "Dinner wasn't very good," she said quickly. "That's all."

"It was fine," he murmured, his lips now just tracing the edge of her ear as he spoke.

"It was not fine," she denied irritably. "The meat was overcooked and the vegetables weren't good and the cake was too sugary." She started to get up from the sofa but the hand that had been toying so gently with her hair had suddenly become a steel clamp on her shoulder.

"It seems to me you started acting this way before dinner, Emma," he said mildly. "I don't remember exactly when, but one minute you were happy to see me and the next you couldn't stand the sight of me. We're going to sit here until you tell me what made you change your mind."

"That's ridiculous," she sputtered, trying unsuccessfully to stand up and only succeeding in kicking the coffee table ineffectually. "You can't make me sit here."

"Of course I can," he answered, reaching across to her leg and in one swift movement pulling her sideways and down so that he lay half on top of her, pinning her to the couch even more firmly. "See?" he grinned, and then seeing Emma's look of alarm, he remembered the purpose of the exercise. "I'm not going to take you by force, if that's what you're afraid of, Em, and I'll let you up now if you want. But what am I supposed to think when my sweet-tempered woman turns sour and won't tell me why? I have to leave for Europe on Monday, and if I'm going to leave in the middle of an argument I want to know what we're fighting about."

"I'm not your woman!" Emma finally exploded in a rage.

He looked stunned. "You're not?"

"No," she said, squirming to sit up and succeeding this time. Simon sat up beside her, his hair tousled and his eyes wary. "You don't need me to speak anymore, remember? You won't be coming up here anymore."

"I can't just come up to see you?" he asked.

Emma sighed impatiently. "Simon, be realistic."

"I am being realistic!" he exploded in turn. "You told me last Saturday you wouldn't speak and I believed you. But I want to keep seeing you," he added in a softer voice.

Emma started to listen to him, started to let her defenses down. "You do?"

He nodded. "I'll come up as soon as I get back from Europe."

"Ah, Europe. I knew there was a hitch."

"Emma, for God's sake, I told you why I have to go, if you were listening to a thing I said at dinner. I'd put it off if I could, but I can't, so I'm going to go on and get it over with." They were sitting stiffly side by side now, careful not to touch, but he turned his head slightly to see her face out of the corner of his eye. "Didn't last night mean anything to you?"

Emma couldn't bring herself to answer immediately. "You know it did," she finally said in a choked whisper.

"Then why are you putting up such a fight? You think this kind of thing happens to me every weekend? I have a new woman for every project?"

"I don't know," she mumbled.

"Well, I don't," he said firmly and then softened. "Last night was a little out of character for both of us, wasn't it?"

"Yes." What he was saying made her feel better, but she still felt like squirming away and crawling into a hole to hide.

"So if I tell you I'm going to come back on Memorial Day weekend, will you believe me?"

She hesitated. "I believe you mean what you say."

He reached out and caught her face in one huge hand, squeezing her cheeks so that her lips puckered out in a pout like a baby's. "Emma, I'm going to see you on the twenty-ninth, and I'm going to teach you how to swim."

"No, you're not."

"Yes, I am, dammit."

"Simon, this hurts," she said between her scrunched-up cheeks.

"Sorry," he said, releasing her and standing up. "I'd better go. If I'm leaving on Monday I've got a lot to do, and I don't think we're going to accomplish too much here tonight."

Emma stood up and walked him to the door. "Have a nice trip," she said awkwardly.

"Gee, thanks. I'm sure to now." She looked up quickly to read his expression and saw just a flicker of a teasing glint in his eyes. "Goodbye, Em. I'll see you in three weeks at the latest." He reached out for her shoulders, but instead of kissing her he pulled her to him and wrapped his arms around her in a tight bear hug, pinning her arms to her sides and half lifting her off the floor. It was a hug full of rage and frustration, and lasted until Emma could sense the first stirrings of passion, but he released her then and put her firmly away from him before he could act on his own impulses. By the time she was steady on her feet again, he was gone.

She turned away and slowly finished straightening up and getting ready for bed. One thing was certain—she had never truly been hugged before tonight. In fact, she wished he hadn't let go of her quite so soon. She had liked the feel of his hardening body even though the position he held her in made it impossible to respond, and she wondered why he had been so hasty to push her away and leave. When he had left her last weekend, she had also wanted him to stay and make love to her, but she had been afraid to suggest it. And now, even after what had happened between them, she still was.

She was tired of this feeling of insecurity she was burdened with, she thought as she sat heavily on the side of the bed in her old nightgown. Surely it was time all those ghosts from her first marriage were laid to rest. And surely the way to do it was with another man, a nice man.

Simon was certainly nice, even when he was trying to be harsh. She thought about when he had squeezed her cheeks to make her look at him. Funny, but she hadn't minded in the least, even when it started to hurt a little. He simply forgot the strength of his own flesh and the relative frailty of hers. It was a contrast she found appealing, and she thought again how much she wished he had stayed.

Perhaps if he had made love to her he would have felt more strongly bound to her, obligated to come back to her after his trip. On the other hand, since he hadn't, maybe he would feel he now had something to come back *for*. Emma realized the turn her thoughts had taken and fluffed her pillow angrily. Why was it so difficult for her to stop thinking like that, as though making love—having sex, she corrected herself—was in some strange way a commodity. She had been taught it was a gift to bestow on one special man, and it was certainly a giving of oneself, but the giving did not insure anything in return. So the only answer was that if Simon wanted to come back, he would, and there was nothing she could do about it in the meantime.

She turned her head and glanced at the clock. It was not quite eleven. The desk at the Lyon's Inn was still open, and Simon had a telephone in his room. There was, she realized, something she could do. She had not been particularly welcoming of either him or his earlier embraces that evening, and now that she had had a chance to reflect, she was sorry. She had behaved like a temperamental idiot. She *was* a temperamental idiot, she corrected herself, and Simon had been nothing but sweet in response, and she decided she would like to call him and say good-night nicely. It was possible he would still like to come over, although since he would be the one to get up and into his clothes, she thought she would let him suggest that. There was no time to think about it any longer, so she quickly looked up the number and dialed the inn.

"Mr. Simon Eliot isn't here, ma'am," the voice on the other end informed her, and she thought she detected just a hint of pleasure in the lackadaisical tone. She would have thought he saw enough intrigue that her own discreet little affair would have held no interest for him.

"What do you mean he isn't there?" she pressed, wondering if he knew someone else in town or was just out wandering. "Has he come back yet tonight?"

"Mr. Eliot checked out this afternoon."

Emma hung up the receiver and leaned back against her pillows. Checked out, had he? That could mean one of two things. Either he had intended to stay with her that night, or he had never intended to stay in Litchfield, had in fact intended for things to happen just as they did. And she would never know which.

An old maxim of her mother's came unbidden to mind. You can never know a man's intentions until he asks you to marry him. It was one of a long list that had been drummed into her head for as long as she could remember, a series of spells intended to ward off evil. If she obeyed she would be safe, and although she had already broken quite a few, she could never contravene one without hearing the rule being chanted in her mother's voice. It was a legacy, even though her mother was still very much alive. Emma wondered what kinds of advice she would pass on to her children if she had any, little tidbits of wisdom that dropped from her lips almost unconsciously. When she fell asleep she had a strange, mixed-up dream about a community of women that were being threatened by a dark man with huge hands, and she felt guilty all through the dream because she hoped the man would win, although she could tell the women were trying to protect her.

The digital clock on Simon's bedside table read 8:29 when he finally decided he had waited long enough. He picked up the telephone and punched the button he had already programmed to dial Emma's number. Even if he had had a place to stay the night, he would have left Litchfield after his dinner with Emma. He had been so annoyed that the thought of going to bed had been out of the question, and he was afraid if he stayed in town he would forget the very good reasons he had for not trying to make love to her.

He had told himself almost all the way home that he didn't want to rush her, did not want to push her into a relationship she wasn't ready for. There seemed to be a frailty about her that he found almost terrifying, and he was afraid if he forced anything on her she would break. It wasn't until he was pulling into the garage under his Manhattan apartment, absently inserting his key in the lock and waiting for the door to open, that the truth had begun to glimmer in his confused mind.

He was the one who was afraid of rushing into a relationship. He was the one whose emotions were fairly terrifying in their intensity, and next to his own suddenly shaken world, Emma had the stability of the Rock of Gibraltar.

The evening, once he forced himself to study it, was chock full of revealing material, the most shocking being that he wanted some sort of "relationship" with Emma. It was a word he had never associated with himself before. He didn't consider himself promiscuous, but neither did he consider himself possessive, and if a woman

he was sufficiently friendly with to make love to found
herself in bed with another man, well, he would catch her
another time. He didn't like making a lot of plans in advance, preferring to act on an impulse of the moment
rather than being tied down to any certain future.

Why, then, had he made definite plans to see Emma as
soon as he got back from Europe? He'd been looking
forward to the freedom of a jaunt to France, hoping to
clear his mind of his complicated feelings for this woman,
and taking more time there than he really needed; instead he had deliberately chosen to carry her image with
him the whole way. He'd just started to tell himself he
was not, however, committed to anything when a new
fear gripped him. What if she didn't want to see him? She
hadn't exactly been overwhelmed by passion the night
before, and she'd been as surprised as he had to hear
himself calling her "his" woman. The only thing he
could think of now was the fact that she had denied it.

This disquieting memory had troubled the remaining
hours of the night. He had wanted to phone her immediately for reassurance, but he forced himself to wait, and
by the time it was light out he had not only managed to
doze off, but he had a firmer grip on himself. It wouldn't
do at all to let her know how he felt at this point, and
perhaps after a few weeks of indulgence in all the dis-
tractions Paris had to offer, his ardor would have cooled.
All the same, it couldn't hurt just to check.

The telephone rang four times before he heard Emma's husky voice murmur a sleepy "hello."

"Sorry to wake you." He had a vivid mental image of
her lying naked in the crumpled sheets, her wavy hair
spread across the pillow, her limbs heavy and relaxed with
sleep. No, she probably wore a nightie when she wasn't

sleeping with him. He would have to see if he could change that.

"No. Yes. Yes, you did wake me," Emma answered, coming slowly to her senses.

"I know I did. It's awfully late to still be asleep. Didn't you go to bed after I left?"

"I didn't sleep very well," she mumbled, sounding resentful.

"Didn't you? Emma, wake up. Stand up and jump up and down, or something. I want to ask you a question."

She groaned softly and he could hear the rustle of sheets. "I'm standing. I refuse to jump. What do you want? Where are you?"

"I'm in New York. Emma—"

"Why?" she interrupted.

"Because I didn't feel like going to sleep and I decided to go on and drive home. Listen, Em, it occurs to me that I was a little too forceful last night."

"That's okay," she said. Far from it, she thought.

"I never gave you a chance to tell me whether or not you wanted to keep seeing me."

"Oh," she said, taken aback. She didn't think about her answer at all. "Yes, of course I do."

"Are you sure?"

Never tell a man how you feel about him, her mother's voice whispered. "Yes, I'm sure."

"Well, then, everything's fine." He sounded relieved, even to himself. "Listen, I've got to get to the office. I'll talk to you when I get back and I'll see you at the end of the month."

"Right. Have a nice trip," Emma answered softly and then, when he had hung up, she sat back down on the bed as though she had been released from a spell. She had a little trouble believing she had actually just spoken to him, after the way she had been feeling last night. Apparently everything was indeed fine, and she had been worried for nothing. She was up and half-dressed for breakfast with Stu before she started having doubts again. Were they committed to each other now? Of course she wanted to keep seeing him, but would that mean the same thing to him as it did to her? She wished she had played it a little safer, been a little cooler, suggested they not make definite plans and see how they felt when he got back. She could always be a little standoffish when he came back. If he came back.

When she went outside and walked up Main Street to the restaurant she had a curious, floating feeling, as though some invisible source of support she had been unconsciously relying on had been removed and she was just managing to stay up by herself.

Seven

When Emma came to her senses the next Monday and realized that almost an entire week of May had slipped by without her noticing, she was appalled. She had not even remarked on the passing of May Day, which she usually celebrated with fresh flowers in the studio and a brief rundown of the history of the pagan celebration on the air. Emma was a person who paid attention to details, and in losing a week of spring, she felt as though she had lost something real. She decided this was Simon's fault.

When he had telephoned the morning before, he had caught her in a vulnerable state, and while she realized she had not admitted to anything incriminating—saying that she wanted to see him again did not give him any particular rights over her—she found herself resenting him for even forcing that simple admission out of her. She did not know what she would have been feeling if he had not called. She had been suspicious of his reasons for

checking out of his hotel early, and if he had left her ig-
norant of the reason, left her with only their unsatisfactory conversation in her apartment and that memorable
hug, she would have been able to spend three entire weeks
pondering their future and doubting the purity of his intentions. She supposed she might have been able to talk
herself out of having any faith in him altogether. She was
by nature a trusting soul, but she had developed a few
healthy suspicions of people over the years, and her instincts were telling her to be wary of Simon.

The problem with his phone call was that now there
was nothing for her suspicions to latch on to. She reminded herself that every time she had doubted him, he
had come through. He had always been fair and honest.
He had passed up opportunities to seduce her when he
didn't think she was ready. The tawdry scene in his hotel
room (she persisted in associating the word "tawdry"
with the act of going to bed with a man one had known
for only one week) was certainly as much her fault as his,
if not more so. He was being completely honorable, and
the only problem was that she was afraid if she started
totally believing in him, he would disappear. He was the
opposite of the tooth fairy: doubting him was more likely
to keep him steadfast. The best thing she could possibly
do was convince herself that she didn't care about him.

It was with more than her customary enthusiasm,
therefore, that she threw herself into the preparations for
the annual Memorial Day Festival on the Green, which
the radio station had sponsored for the past five years.
Litchfield, like many New England towns, had a long,
beautiful, shady central green that had held the festival
since Emma had first conceived of the need for one. It
traditionally took place on Saturday, and the first part of
the day was given over to a glorious mixture of craft fair,

flea market and bake sale. The quality of goods at the various "stands," as they were called, usually consisting of a few card tables, was high as each resident vied with the other for customers. The only rules were that you had to be a Litchfield resident and you had to get your name on the list in time, as space was, naturally, limited. Emma had been afraid the first year that people would simply use the opportunity to clean out their cellars, but she needn't have worried. Snob appeal was strong in the little town, and while a collection of comic books was tolerated if it was a really good collection, wares generally were more along the line of handmade quilts or a display of antique milk glass that the owner simply had no room for.

The gourmet foods section, which catered almost exclusively to the sweet tooth, was another main attraction. While the town's commercial baker always had his own stand, he could rarely outdo the truffles handdipped by his neighbor in the hardware store, and Enid Water's fudge brownies always sold out, not because they were particularly good, but because Litchfield had a certain amount of town pride in the fact that their ninety-year-old resident could still bake brownies.

After filling up on cakes, cookies and candies, the festivalgoer then moved on to the barbecue, where for three dollars he or she received a hamburger with fixings, a cold soda, and as many scoops of ice cream as could be consumed. It was another tradition that this was the first barbecue of the season, and considered treasonous to light up the charcoal in your own back yard before Memorial Day weekend.

By the time the light began to fade, the crowd gradually began to thin as people walked home, showered and changed, took a little antacid depending on the extent of their indulgence, and returned to the green, where a platform and a huge, striped tent had been erected between the trees at the south end. This was the part of the festival that Emma liked best. While throughout the afternoon a local band had played a selection of bluegrass and folk and soft rock music, once the stars were out everyone's attention turned to dancing. The year before, she had discovered a band composed of people from all over the state that played swing music with a surprisingly good, big-band sound. She felt a little guilty for not insisting on her "Litchfield only" rule here as well, but she justified herself by not making particularly public just where the "Swinging Syncopaters" came from. They were good, and no one seemed to care.

With all of her preparations to keep her busy, as well as her normal duties at the station, she was hoping to have very little time left over for mooning over Simon's absence and examining in depth every sentence and every kiss they had ever exchanged. It was surprising how often she found herself staring into space with a foolish look on her face, however, and she had to force herself to concentrate on the task of borrowing tables from every church in the area. If someone had told her two weeks before that she would be having this problem, she would have scoffed, and she reminded herself firmly that she was taking the events of two weekends much too seriously. It wasn't until she had what she used to refer to as an Incident with Tony that she realized she had no choice.

By the Saturday before the festival, Emma had done everything that could possibly be done in advance preparation. Food had been ordered, music had been lined up, the list of sellers was full to overflowing, even the weather forecast had been anxiously researched. It had been raining fitfully all day and by evening had settled into a steady downpour. Emma didn't mind. She was confident the weather would get rain out of its system by this time next week, and in the meantime was content to spend an evening at home, a Bach cantata on the stereo, newspapers spread out on the floor of the kitchen and a lump of wet clay between her hands.

Another discovery Emma had made about herself after her divorce, a time of both pleasant and painful discoveries, was that she could do just about anything with her hands that she set out to do. A sympathizing friend of her mother's had sent a pattern for a crewelwork pillow cover that she had taken to immediately, and after several years of presenting the members of her family with lovely but mostly useless bits of stitchery, she had turned to pottery. Although she had to send her various creations to a kiln in Danbury, the Litchfield craft store supplied her with glazes and clay and everything else she needed.

Tonight she had come home and slipped an old, stained man's shirt over her clothes to act as a smock and then set about forming what her hands seemed to want her to form. All she knew was that she wanted the glaze to be a dappled green, but she had yet to decide on such fundamentals as shape, size and identity of object. Percy had seated himself on the windowsill and occasionally raised a lazy paw to bat at the trickling droplets on the pane, but he had seen rain before and could not really bother to be kittenish about it.

It was in the middle of this cozy scene that the doorbell rang. Emma got up off the floor and rinsed her hands hastily in the sink before answering it. It was late enough that the downstairs door should have been locked, so she assumed it was one of the other tenants and was surprised to find Tony's lanky form leaning against the wall across the hall. She was doubly surprised at the despondent look in his normally lively brown eyes.

She opened the door wider and silently motioned him in, watching with a worried look in her green eyes as he sat down wearily on the couch and leaned his head on his hand. "Got any booze?" he asked.

Emma tried not to smile. At the moment he was more than anything like the little brother she never had, although he was two years older than she was, and she suspected he wanted liquor not to drown his sorrows, but to underscore the seriousness of this particular problem. She went into the kitchen and returned with a glass of ice and Simon's bottle of Scotch, hoping he wouldn't want her to join him. Even with only a little alcohol, her hands would not be as coordinated as she would wish, and she hoped that she would have time to return to her pottery after Tony left.

"What's up?" she asked after she felt the sympathetic silence had gone on long enough.

"It's Joanne," he finally announced with a shaky sigh. "It's over."

"Are you sure?" He nodded. "Where is she to-night?"

"Out with some other guy, I guess," he said with a shrug. She watched in alarm as he drained his glass of Scotch, not without a certain amount of effort, and then poured himself another.

"Well, now, Tony, maybe you're overreacting. What happened? Did you have a fight?"

He sighed gustily and sat back, tilting his head against the back of the couch and staring up at the ceiling. Emma took a seat on the other end of the couch, curling her legs up underneath her and turning to face him. They had consoled each other through crises before, and she knew he would tell her what was wrong as soon as he had found the right words. He had not taken particularly well to his high-school education and as a result always chose his words with care, never feeling entirely confident of his ability to express himself. "She doesn't want to get serious," he volunteered. "I don't know, I was counting on seeing her tonight and I guess I thought she was counting on it, too. Turned out that when I called to say when I'd be by for her, she said she wouldn't be there, that she had a 'previous engagement,'" he said, ending with a slight sneer.

"Sounds like you might have been taking her for granted," Emma remarked after considering the problem.

He shook his head. "I wasn't taking her for granted, I just thought she liked me as much as I liked her. I thought we really understood each other, but I guess we don't." He sat up to take a long drink of his Scotch and then lay back against the couch. "I guess I'll never find a woman who understands me," he said in a self-pitying voice. "Except you," he added.

Emma started to smile, reaching out to nudge him with her toe and tease him out of his mood, but his face looked sincerely sorrowful and she changed her tactic, sliding across the couch to put her arms around him and lay his face against her shoulder. It was a scene they had enacted several times before, because Tony's love life never ran particularly smoothly, and he usually turned to her for a little support and a warm hug.

Emma herself found it hard to understand why Tony had such trouble finding a woman to appreciate him. She had never been tempted to deepen their relationship and had no idea how he behaved as a lover, but he was sweet and kind and attractive, his body tall and slim, but with well-defined muscles, blond hair cut short for the sake of comfort, and a perpetual suntan from his work in the National Forest. He had a youthful air about him, and considered that an evening spent drinking beer and staring, with increasingly maudlin appreciation, at the moonlight on nearby Bantam Lake was time well spent. Emma had a limited tolerance for those evenings herself, but suspected that with the right woman, Tony had great potential.

She was lost in these musings, absently patting his shoulder and staring at a cobweb she had just noticed above the kitchen door, when it was brought to her attention that Tony's hand was moving down her arm in a rather unfraternal stroke and his face had moved from the relative innocence of her shoulder to the more sensitive part of her neck. By the time the hand reached the bare skin of her forearm, she was fully aware that the mood had changed and that Tony was in the process of making a pass at her.

"Hey, cut it out," she mumbled, shifting uncomfortably and feeling embarrassed. To her dismay, however, he didn't cut it out, sliding close to her again and putting his head back on her shoulder. She stiffened nervously, uncomfortable now with such close contact.

"Come on, Emma, why can't we just hold each other?" he said, the tone of his voice one she had never heard before. He sounded insinuating, as though he were trying to talk her into doing something naughty before she could figure out what it was.

"Because we don't do that," she said, hesitant to give him any more definite reason.

"Why don't we?" he persisted, starting to slip a hand over her belly. "Joanne and I are through, and your friend from New York hasn't been around lately. Why can't you and I console each other, hmh?''

Emma gave him a vicious shove and jumped up from the couch. "Because I don't want to, Tony," she said, trying not to give in to rage and stamp her foot. "We've been through this before, and if you're my friend, you won't push me like this. Why did you let this happen now? I was just trying to make you feel better and you're taking advantage of me," she finished, almost in tears. They had been through this before, but she wished so strongly that it had been Simon cuddling her on the couch that she could not help overreacting.

Tony stared at her for a moment, taken aback, and then sighed and rose heavily from the couch, moving over to stare out the window. "I'm sorry," he finally said, turning around to look at her but careful to keep his distance. "It's just that sometimes it's hard for me to like you as much as I do and not let it go any further."

"Oh," she said in a small voice, staring at the floor, relieved that the scene was over but still wishing he would leave.

"I'm not a eunuch, you know," he informed her.

"I never thought you were." Emma looked up and saw him leaning back against the wall, a smile finally beginning to grow in his eyes, and she smiled back and began to relax.

"Are you still mad at me?"

"Yes, but I'll try to get over it."

"Well, then, I think I'll leave. You're kind of a pain to be around when you're nursing a grudge," he said as he nonchalantly walked to the door.

"I ought to kick your—" she said in exasperation, rushing after him, but he dodged out of the way and the door slammed in her face. She leaned against it, hearing his feet on the stairs in the echoing silence, and sighed with relief. She had not thought about Tony's reaction to her affair with Simon but he was clearly feeling the strain. It was easier for him to accept that she was simply not interested in men than that she was not interested in him in particular, and although she was still genuinely angry with him for coming on to her tonight, she supposed the whole scene could have been avoided if she had been a little more open with him to begin with.

She turned the record on the stereo over and went back into the kitchen, sitting down on the floor and absently picking up the abandoned clay. It had dried out too much in the interim to be malleable, and she knew she would have to add a little water to it, but she remained on the floor, crumbling it between her fingers, while she thought about her reaction to the tussle on the couch. She had never felt revulsion for Tony before, and theirs had always been a fairly physical friendship, with kisses on the cheek, linked arms while walking through town and an occasional shared blanket when she deigned to join him in his admiration of the moon on the lake. But tonight had been something new, and she wondered if her relationship with Simon was taking its unsuspected toll on any other part of her life.

She closed her eyes and thought back to the way Tony's hand had felt on her arm, and suddenly it became a larger, stronger hand, the arm that imprisoned her body more forceful and the face against her neck slightly grizzled with a five-o'clock shadow. Suddenly Simon was there, guiding her back against the cushions, crushing her with his weight, obliterating her every sensation except delight at the feel of his flesh against hers.

She came back to her senses with a jerk, aware that she was sitting on the floor in her old clothes, dried clay stuck to her palms, her pulse racing and her cheeks flushed. She repressed an urge to berate herself, resignedly standing up to moisten the clay at the sink and sitting back down to try to force it into a recognizable shape. After thirty futile minutes, however, all she had was a strange-looking little pot that was too small to be anything useful and too big to get away with being simply decorative. She crushed it without a qualm and put it back into its container, cleaned up the floor and got ready to go to bed. She didn't know why, and she didn't know whether Tony's visit had anything to do with it or not, but she was not nearly as contented with her solitude as she had been at the beginning of the evening.

At approximately the same time that Emma was reaching her sisterly arm out to Tony, Simon was sitting by himself in a Parisian café, staring in befuddlement at the empty seat opposite him. He was beginning to suspect that the young lady who had recently vacated it had actually been bored by his fascinating company, but he was hard put to understand just why. He had had a long dinner with the director of the Edmonds documentary, during which they had tried to console themselves for failing miserably with Germaine Marque. The old bag, as they had begun calling her, had repeatedly refused to have anything to do with them, and they were both unable to understand how she could resist two such charming fellows. Simon had not paid particular attention to the amount of glasses of wine he had consumed, and could not quite remember just when his friend had gone on his merry way, deciding to try his luck, as he put it, elsewhere and leaving Simon to find what amusement he could in the early hours of the morning at the café across the street from his hotel.

Simon stared at the street thoughtfully. It had occurred to him that eventually he would have to cross it,
but he was not quite ready to venture forward. The
phrase "Wine, women and song" kept running through
his head—he and Jack Morissey had discussed in great
detail the merits of each—and he felt that somehow he
would be doing Paris an injustice if he did not partici-
pate in each one of them. He had planted himself at this
table in search of company, not because he wanted it, but
because he felt it was the thing to do. And, being what he
was, he had already attracted a couple of qualified can-
didates. But for some reason they weren't sticking
around. Simon analyzed his conversation to determine
the reason for this novel, if not particularly pleasant, experience in rejection.

He had only wanted to talk, he hadn't suggested anything lascivious, but both women seemed to grow unac-
countably restless after very promising beginnings.
Perhaps, he thought, Parisian women were more busi-
nesslike when it came to sex and only wanted him to put
up or shut up. This offended him. And then again, perhaps they simply weren't interested in hearing about
Emma. Well, he would never understand women and that
was all there was to it.

He drained the last of his brandy and fished among the
coins in his pocket for what he considered a generous tip.
It never occurred to him that he should pay for the
brandy as well, and the proprietor, who had served him
breakfast that morning and expected to see him again the
next day, decided to let it pass. Although Simon's behavior had been as docile as a lamb, one could never tell
with these big Americans. He watched his progress across
the street with motherly solicitude, impressed that the
cars stopped for him rather than the other way around.

Simon bumped his head on his way into the tiny elevator in his hotel and then stared at the numbers on the panel. After a moment, he looked through the metal cage to the young woman seated at the desk in the lobby.

"Quarante-deux, monsieur," she informed him.

Simon tried to wink at her, which he felt was an appropriate response under the circumstances, but by the time he had managed to work out the complicated movement of his facial muscles, the elevator had come to a stop on his floor. Once in his room, he methodically removed all his clothes, found the plastic telephone-company calling card in his wallet, and set it on the table by the bed, adjusting the lamp so that it shone directly on it. He then made himself comfortable in the bed, mustered all his concentration, and picked up the telephone receiver to begin the laborious job of reading the appropriate numbers to the helpless operator on the other end.

"Quinze," he was saying some minutes later. "No, I don't mean *quinze.* What's the word? Oh, *cinq,* I think it's *cinq...."*

Although it was early for Emma to be in bed, she had just managed to doze off when the telephone rang. She sat upright with a jerk, unsure what had woken her so abruptly, when it rang again. Slightly shaky from the shock, she snatched the receiver off the cradle. "Hello?" she said, half-afraid she would hear bad news on the other end, that one of her parents had had an accident, or the studio was on fire. For the first couple of seconds she didn't hear anything at all, but then if she listened closely she could hear, through the static, a muted roar, a soft sound that built to a crescendo and then turned into a sigh. She concentrated on the sound for a moment. Someone was snoring into her telephone.

Her first thought was that it might be Tony, but while he was a great one for playing pranks, she thought this was a little out of character. It also sounded like long distance, and she couldn't imagine who would go to the trouble and expense of making anonymous long-distance phone calls and then not even bother to make them obscene. She knew instinctively that this was no ordinary heavy breather. She listened for a moment or two, finding the sound oddly peaceful, and then gently replaced the receiver in the cradle, quietly, so that she wouldn't wake whoever was on the other end.

Emma shaded her eyes against the setting sun and watched a workman finish hammering down the last platform of the dance floor. It was covered by an enormous tent of cheerful blue and white, but it was possible to see definite signs of wear on the fabric where it stretched over the corner poles, and she hoped that she would be able to find enough money in the treasury after the festival to afford a new one. It was doubtful if this one had another season in it.

She turned away with a sigh. There was never quite enough money; she was always having to scrape pennies together, deny herself or the station some little needed improvement, hand out measly little salaries to her employees. Actually they were partners rather than employees, she reminded herself, now that she had instituted a profit-sharing plan. They had chosen that option over an admittedly small cost-of-living increase in their wages, after Emma had opened the books to them and explained the situation very frankly. The station had always been strapped financially—it was part and parcel of running a small business—but lately she had less tolerance for the constant worry of budgeting herself.

She had less tolerance for a lot of things, she reflected as she looked over the crowded green and listened to the laughter and the raucous sounds of people having a good time. She had participated earlier, even trying one of Enid's brownies, but as her tongue first explored the overly sweet, heavy lump in her palm she had had to repress a shudder, and she wondered, as she discreetly wrapped it up and threw it into a garbage can, just what Enid had put in them this year. The other stands had not been much more rewarding, and she suspected, as she wandered among silver-plated cake stands and hand-crocheted lace tablecloths, that she had seen at least half these items before.

But that didn't matter, she told herself angrily. That wasn't the point of this little gathering. The point was for the town to come together and have fun, swap stories, gossip. And that was exactly what everybody was doing except her. And why? She clenched her fists. Why? Because of Simon Eliot, blast his hide. She had not heard one single word from him, not even a postcard, although she wasn't sure what he could have said on a postcard, anyway—"Having a wonderful time. About next weekend, let's just forget it."

Her response had been to wait around the apartment the day before and this morning, glaring at the very silent telephone, even lowering herself to check for messages at the studio, and then when she finally had to leave, she had wandered around in a sulk and refused to get involved in the party. *Her* party. Tony had decided she was still angry after last weekend and was busy ignoring her, squiring around some young blond girl that Emma had hated at first sight.

"There is always something better to do than feel sorry for yourself," her mother's voice reminded her in one of her rare tidbits of good advice, and Emma straightened her shoulders unconsciously and approached a familiar-looking van. The "Swinging Syncopaters" had just arrived, and she wanted to make sure they had everything they needed to set up.

Five hours later Emma was still standing beneath a broad oak tree, watching the party from a distance. She had gone home to freshen up and change into a skirt when everybody else did, and she was half wishing she had not come back. She had always loved this part of the evening, loved the music, dragged anybody she could commandeer onto the dance floor, but for some reason it seemed unbearably romantic tonight. She didn't think she could stand to dance with somebody else's husband, or feel some strange man's pudgy arm squeezing her waist too tightly, not when the stars were so clear and the wind in the dark leaves overhead was a soft whisper, just audible between songs. She wished briefly that she had hired a rock band this year, anything but this heartrending, evocative music that made her body want to dance when her heart wasn't up to it.

It was almost over. The band was playing their last set, and she felt she ought to stay and make sure everything ran smoothly, that kids didn't loiter on the green, that the grass wasn't full of litter. She was pleased with herself for having gone the distance, even if she had lurked in the shadows most of the night as though she had some guilty secret. It hadn't been easy, and she was half looking forward to going home and, for the first time, indulging in a bout of self-pity, but she had to keep a grip on herself just a little longer.

She shifted her weight restlessly, letting her gaze run idly over the scene before her, and without warning her senses came alive with a jolt and her heart started beating with a painful thud. There was a man standing just a few feet away from her, looking over the dance floor, and every nerve in her body recognized him. He was wearing a rumpled, dark business suit, the knot of his tie loosened slightly and the top button of his shirt open; an overnight bag was slung over his shoulder, and a shaggy lock of hair had fallen over his forehead. There was something weary in the set of his shoulders, and she thought even in the dark, from a distance, that his face looked tired. And then he looked over and saw her, drawn somehow by her gaze, and instantly his demeanor changed.

"There you are," he said, coming over to her and starting to kiss her, and then halting, his hands still on her shoulders, hesitant in the face of her stillness.

"I...thought you weren't coming," she volunteered after staring up at him for a moment. Her eyes memorized every detail of his face with loving attention, and she wanted to reach up her hand to stroke his cheek, but she didn't.

Simon was struggling to restrain himself, wanting nothing more than to pull her against him, wrap his arms around her luscious body and kiss her until neither one of them could breathe anymore. It was what he had been looking forward to for three weeks, and now for some reason he was almost afraid to, feeling instead some crazy compulsion to make conversation. "I just got in four hours ago. I tried to call from the airport, but you weren't home, so I came on ahead. We have a date, don't we?"

"Yes," she said in a voice that was increasingly husky. She resolutely quelled an urge to press herself against his firm chest and tangle her fingers in the hair that brushed his collar.

"How much longer does this party go on?" he asked.

"They're almost finished," she said, tearing her gaze away to glance at her watch. "This is the last set."

"Then we should make the most of it, shouldn't we?" he asked, pulling her over to the dance floor. He was bone tired, didn't really feel much like dancing, but he wanted his arms around Emma, and the music was enticing.

As they stepped onto the platform, the band launched into the sweet strains of "Moonlight Serenade," the final number, and a strange feeling of unreality settled over Emma as she went into his arms. This was what she had been waiting for, this was the only thing she wanted, and she could not believe it was happening. They moved together a little stiffly at first, but then the music took over, and abandoning the pretence that they were any ordinary couple, they pulled each other into a tighter embrace, letting their bodies communicate in a language that words could not match.

Emma tilted her head back once to look up into his face and saw that he was dancing with his eyes closed. Feeling her movement, he pressed her against him again, bending his face down to nuzzle her head into his shoulder and taking advantage of the opportunity to bury his lips in her hair. After a moment he started humming along, and she smiled into the fabric of his jacket, loving the feel of his rumbly baritone in her ear, delighted he had abandoned himself to that extent. They were on the very edge of the crowd of dancers, in their own tiny little circle, and Emma kept her face buried against him, letting him surround all of her senses, unwilling for anything to intrude on the magic.

When the song finally came to an end and the couples on the dance floor stepped away from each other to applaud, Simon kept his arm tight around her waist and stepped away from the lights. "Let's leave," he murmured in her ear, taking her consent for granted as he started walking with her back to the street. And Emma went with him weakly. She was floating. She had, somewhere along the line, abandoned her corporeal form and was skimming over the grass, her direction determined completely by the more stable form next to hers. She was a sprite, she was the nymph he had compared her to earlier, and she managed to spirit them both home without either of them being aware of forward progress.

Eight

——

The magic didn't end. When Simon locked the door behind him and Emma switched on a tiny porcelain lamp next to the couch, the light cast a dim circle that held them in, held out the rest of the night. Simon stood with his back to the door, and while she was unable to see his features, the burning intensity of his eyes drew her, and she drifted to him until her hands were resting on his chest, giving in to that natural, inexorable pull. He shuddered slightly at her touch but made no other move, and finally Emma stood on tiptoe and put a hand behind his head to pull his lips down to hers.

At that something seemed to snap in his rigid self-control. He pulled her against him fiercely, and suddenly his mouth was everywhere, sliding off her lips to plunder the soft flesh of her neck, moving up through her hair and finally returning to her mouth, his tongue moving easily between her lips to the moist recesses beyond.

Emma didn't know how it happened, but she found her own back against the door, her body pinned firmly by Simon's hips while he used his hands to better advantage, unbuttoning her blouse, and when he couldn't unfasten her bra, simply pulling it down to hang around her waist. His lips had been tracing the line of her chin, but when her breasts were free, the nipples like tightly furled rosebuds grazing the front of his shirt, he cupped them in his hands and leaned down to swirl his tongue around one and then devour it like a starving man.

Emma had barely had a chance to respond to his unleashed passion, but now she struggled out of her bra and then began clumsily pulling at the knot in his tie and unbuttoning his shirt. Simon didn't help her any. He was intent only on tasting every bare inch of her flesh, running his hands up under her skirt to slip his fingers into her panties, seemingly oblivious of the fact that they were still in the living room and that Emma was having difficulty taking his clothes off. He had been anticipating this moment for too long, and only came partially to his senses when his roving hand found the sensitive flesh between her thighs, and her legs started to give way.

"Simon," she gasped, clutching his shoulder desperately for balance.

He caught her weight in his arms, lifting her up, and turned to lay her gently on the floor, but then the moment passed, the gentleness was gone, and he was once again moving his mouth over her bare stomach with savage pleasure. Emma had succeeded in unbuttoning his shirt halfway before she became distracted, but she was wearing only her skirt, which was full and slightly filmy and, at the moment, hiked up over one hip. She looked wild, sprawled on the floor, her lips hungry for him, her nipples aroused and obviously aching, and Simon drove his swollen manhood against her surging hips with reckless abandon. His every move was uncalculated and un-controlled and Emma suddenly gave in, stopped trying to impose any particular set of rules over the wild man who seemed bent on possessing her body. If he wanted to make love to her with his tie still hanging around his neck, she thought incoherently, far be it for her to try to stop him.

Somehow, without her help, he managed to take his pants off. She felt his tongue running over her thighs and she reached down frantically to direct him but he wouldn't let her, plunging his tongue into her without warning and then teasing the tiny bud of sensation with his lips. And then he was on top of her, sliding between her legs and grasping the flesh of her hips to hold her still for his penetration. "Em," he groaned in her ear as he slid into her satiny depths. She shivered and clutched his back and then ran her hands down to press him against her, welcoming his thrusts with growing intensity. She could feel her flesh responding to him, drawing him in with deepening shudders, and when her pleasure began to reach a peak, she was half-afraid of her own reaction. She clapped her hand over her mouth but Simon pushed it away and covered her lips with his so that she moaned her pleasure against his mouth, letting him hear and see and taste everything.

His passion fueled by hers, his own climax wasn't long in coming, and when her shudders finally began to die down, he buried his face in her hair and moaned his own fulfillment. It was a long time before either of them could breathe normally. They continued to sprawl on the floor of Emma's prim little sitting room, her skirt tangled around her waist, and Simon clad only in one sock and a formerly crisp, white, button-down business shirt. His tie was crushed between their bodies and would never be the same.

The first thing that Emma was aware of was the discreet ticking of the little antique clock that sat on the mantle. Everything else was deathly quiet with the exception of a heartbeat, but she couldn't tell if it was hers or Simon's. She wondered idly if they had managed to disturb any of her neighbors, but this was an old house, with thick walls, and she couldn't quite bring herself to mind even if they had. No one, she decided, would believe that the unearthly moans she suspected she had uttered had actually come from her apartment. She tried to adjust herself to avoid a button that was digging into her back, but she was still pinned to the floor by Simon's heavy body, and he didn't appear to be willing to let her up just yet.

He slowly raised his head, looking as though he were returning from a different state of consciousness altogether. "Are you—" he began and then stopped to clear his throat, not quite succeeding in dispelling the huskiness from his voice. "Are you all right?"

"Yes," she answered.

"I'm sorry, I've been behaving like a cave man."

This time he was met with a dazzling smile. "Yes," she agreed.

He started to smile back uncertainly. "I didn't hurt you, did I?"

"No, not at all." Her voice was a soft, velvety purr and prompted him to raise up slightly and support himself on his elbows so that he could study her more effectively. Her eyes were wide and greener than usual, her cheeks were flushed and her lips were still slightly swollen. She looked warm and soft and satisfied, and Simon began growing excited again just at the sight of her. He moved away and pulled her into his arms, standing up to cradle her against his chest. "What are you doing?" she asked, still feeling limp and curiously delicate.

"I'm putting you to bed," he said, moving smoothly into the bedroom and laying her down so that he could pull her skirt off her hips. "I've been thinking about this for three weeks, and this time I intend to do it right."

"You've been doing just fine," she murmured lazily, reaching out for him as he stood over her, taking off his shirt. And Simon, despite the best of intentions, never got around to removing his other sock.

Emma woke up long before Simon did the next morning. She curled up next to him while he was still deeply asleep and studied the lines of his face, remembering the first time she had seen him. She had been drawn to him even then, standing there wishing in spite of everything she knew was wise that he would wake up. Now she was content to have him sleep, however, so that she could marvel in peace at the fact that he was here in her bed, that he had, apparently, missed her.

All her attempts to forget about him these past weeks had been foolish and futile, she realized now. She was in love with him. And while she didn't know just exactly what that meant, or whether it was good or bad, she knew it was the truth. She propped herself up on one elbow and looked at the way his face was half-buried in the pillow and one bare shoulder appeared above the sheet, looking curiously youthful, almost frail. That was ironic, she thought with amusement. There was absolutely nothing frail about the long male body next to hers. He had taken her, ravished her, three times last night, making her feel thoroughly loved, wanted, needed. He had behaved as though he wanted to permanently merge their two bodies, to encompass as well as penetrate, to know completely every crevasse and curve, and Emma found that she adored him slavishly. She felt reborn into a new self, and she stretched luxuriantly in the bed, enjoying the unfamiliar sensation of the cool sheets slipping over her naked flesh.

Since Simon had finally admitted to having been up for thirty hours, she was careful not to wake him as she slid out of bed and headed for the shower. She stood under the hot spray for a long time and when she finally emerged, warm and pink, she pulled on a summery cotton robe, combed her hair, and started her coffee maker. She was still sitting at the kitchen table poring over the pages of *Newsweek*, her hair beginning to dry and form its customary curls, when she began hearing signs of life from the vicinity of the bedroom.

The first indication was the rustling of sheets, and then a sleepy sounding "Em?"

"Hmmm?" she answered, half closing her eyes and smiling, relishing the sensation.

"Come back in here," she was commanded. She rose and walked into the bedroom to find that Simon had kicked the sheets onto the floor and was lying on his back in naked splendor, his feet hanging over the end of the bed. His baby-blue eyes were half closed, he badly needed a shave, and when he held out an arm for her to join him, she sat down next to him without hesitation. He immediately pulled her down beside him and held her down with a long, naked leg. "Morning," he mumbled into her damp curls. He smelled musky and sweaty, and she thought she could just catch a lingering whiff of aftershave. Emma decided he smelled like France, and turned to bury her face in the base of his throat and inhale deeply. "What's the verdict?" he asked. "Do I need a shower or can I wait a few more days?"

"You can wait as long as you like, but I wouldn't go into polite company if I were you."

"Aren't you polite?" She smiled and shook her head. He stared down at her for a minute, his head propped up on an elbow. "You're just trying to distract me so I'll forget about your swimming lesson."

"It's too cold to swim today, Simon," she said confidently.

"No, it isn't. The lake is open for business; it's Memorial Day weekend."

"Well, that doesn't mean it's warm enough," she protested.

"Of course it does. You must leave these things in the hands of higher authorities and not try to determine for yourself whether or not it's warm enough to go swimming. The lake is open, ergo it is time to learn to swim," he pronounced, amused at her increasing discomfort. "What's the matter, don't you have a swimsuit?"

"Of course I do," she said, wishing she had made a point to cut the tags off already. She had bought one just in case he made good on his threat, but she didn't want him to know that.

"Is it one of those things with a steel-plated top and little boxer shorts that come halfway to your knees?"

She squirmed. "No." In fact it had only the thinnest layer of support in the bodice and was cut much too high on the hip to suit her, but Stu had talked her into it.

"Then what's the problem?"

Emma sighed. She was beaten. "Problem? Who said there's a problem?"

A couple of hours later, as she stood ankle deep in the cold waters of Lake Waramaug, Emma wished she had tried a little harder to talk him out of it. Surely she could have found some sort of delaying tactic, although after watching Simon run into the chill water with a whoop and swim out to the float with long, firm strokes, she doubted it. She shivered and took one more step. She felt almost naked in her swimsuit, and while it was in fact a fairly modest one piece, of a shimmering emerald green, Emma's own figure and the glow that still surrounded her would have made her look alluring in a padded snow suit.

By now the water was lapping at her knees and if she concentrated she could just make out, through the murky lake, her pale toes as they slowly became embedded in goo. She suppressed a shudder of disgust and started to turn back to shore when she realized that Simon had stealthily swum back and was walking toward her with a determined look on his face.

"I don't want to," she said in a small voice.

"Everybody should know how to swim, Emma," he said calmly, as though he were gentling a recalcitrant mare. "It's a good sport and it could save your life some day. Think of all the things you can do once you realize you can swim—sailing, surfing, windsurfing. All you have to do is relax and let the water hold you up." He had taken her arm by now and was firmly pulling her into deeper water.

"But it doesn't hold me up, remember?" she balked, digging her heels in and starting to pull back from him, still unwilling to rebel openly.

"It will. You can float, I can tell just by looking at you."

"What's that supposed to mean?" she asked, perfectly willing to pick a fight if it meant he would let go of her. The water was now soaking the bottom of her suit, and she was leaning back at a sharp angle, when her wishes came true with a vengeance. He let go of her arm and she fell into the water with a resounding splash, catching herself on her hands and her bottom and getting wet to the top of her head. "What did you do that for?" she sputtered in a fury.

"You can't swim without getting wet," he said, standing over her and laughing. "That's the first step."

It was his cavalier attitude that did it. She glared at him for a second, thinking that his teeth were flashing rather wickedly in the sunlight and that his laughter had an evil ring to it, and without thinking of the consequences, she curled her fingers around a large chunk of lake-bottom goo and lunged at him.

"Whoa!" he said, laughing even more gleefully and deflecting the oncoming missile with a careless hand. "Ready for deep water already, huh?" He caught her by the elbows and slowly started towing her out toward the center of the lake.

"No, I'm not," she replied, starting to panic. "What are you doing?"

"Relax, you can still touch the bottom," he said, stopping while she awkwardly let her feet settle. "See?"

She stood facing him, still afraid but feeling slightly calmer now that she was actually standing in the water and still unhurt. "Okay, where do we start?"

"I'm going to put my hand on your back to support you, and you're going to lean back on the water." He did as he said, taking her shoulder in his other hand and gently but relentlessly forcing her back. Emma felt her feet drifting up, and she closed her eyes and prepared to die, but when she opened them a moment later she was, in fact, floating on her back and had a clear view of the sky. Simon had, true to his word, kept his hand on her back, but she could tell that it was the water that was actually holding her.

"I'm floating," she said, delighted with herself and with the sensation.

"I'm going to take my hand away," he said.

"I wish you wouldn't."

"Why not? You won't sink."

"I know," she answered. "But I feel like something is going to reach up and grab me from underneath."

"Like what?"

"I have no idea. That's what I don't like about it."

By now Simon had removed his hand and she looked at him warily out of the corner of her eye. "It's still underneath you, it's just not touching you anymore. But now you know that if you ever need to stop and float, you'll be able to."

"Okay," she said, taking a deep breath and forcing herself to relax. She had no sooner exhaled than there was a flurry of dark water near her foot and a definite pinch in her ankle. She let out a startled gasp, kicked violently, swallowed a mouthful of water and started to go under before Simon caught her and held her firmly against his chest. "What was it?" she asked in a choked voice, both arms wound tightly around his neck.

"You tell me," he said, still daring to look amused at the woman in his arms.

"Something pinched my ankle," she answered, outraged.

"Oh, there is one thing I forgot to tell you about this lake." She looked up at him, her eyes wide, as she noted with relief that he was carrying her back to the shore. "There are fish in it." She looked down at the water and shuddered. He tightened his arms and smiled down at her. "That's probably what bit you."

"Oh." She was beginning to feel a little silly.

"Don't worry, you did just fine. Next time you'll do even better."

"There's going to be a next time?" she asked as he set her down on top of a picnic table.

"It's a long summer, Em," he answered with a grin as he picked up a towel and started drying her feet.

It was a perfect day, cool in the shade and hot in the sun, but after her dip in the lake she was glad to towel herself off and throw a shirt loosely around her shoul-

ders. They ate a picnic lunch and she sat idly sucking a
pear and staring out at the water while Simon dozed on
a blanket in the grass at her feet, having been unable to
fight drowsiness after too little sleep and a brisk swim.
She hoped he wouldn't try to give her lesson number two
this afternoon. Her skin was cool to the touch, but she
felt warm and dry and perfectly satisfied, physically re-
plete and not at all interested in doing any more than admiring the lake from a distance.

And it was certainly a beautiful lake. It was enormous
and surrounded by low hills that were dotted with country inns and beautiful old homes. There was a public park
along one portion of the shore, a wide, flat area shaded
by pine trees, where she and Simon had enjoyed their
lunch, but as far as she could tell they were the only in-
habitants. There was a water skier in the distance, too far
away for her to make out any features, and a couple of
sailboats down near the boat house at the far end, but
there was little wind and they weren't moving very fast.

It was a moment that was simple and serene, but as
Emma stared out at the water, a feeling of nervousness
began to grip her, making her conscious of a queasiness
before she had had time to determine the source. Her
morning at the lake had been idyllic, and idylls were de-
fined by the fact that they never lasted. Something had
to change eventually, and she wondered when Simon was
going to get tired of coming to see her. He had been
wonderfully accommodating so far, appearing as if by
magic to amuse, entertain and love her, and then drop-
ping out of her life again, leaving everything nominally
the same. She wondered if she was being selfish to want
it to go on this way, wondered how long two people with
such different needs and desires could make each other
happy. She wanted to keep him in her world—she did not
want to be in his.

She was gazing at him possessively, the lines of his face both familiar and strange, when his eyelids quivered and he woke up and looked at her. "Have I been asleep long?"

"No," she answered, her voice low and full of sweetness.

He reached up and drew her down to lie on her side, facing him. "You look as if you've been worrying about something." Her only answer was to let him study her face with his penetrating gaze, his blue eyes moving over each feature before settling on hers as though he could read her every thought. "Your eyes aren't sparkling anymore and that smooth forehead has a little line on it." He reached up to smooth the line away with one finger, then let the finger travel irresistibly down to her lips, stroking their fullness and urging them apart. "Everything is going to be fine, don't you know that?" he asked, his voice lowering to a whisper. "With what we've had so far, how can the rest not be just as good or better?"

"But it gets complicated, Simon," she answered, her voice betraying that she was suddenly afraid.

"Only if you let it." His hand tightened on the back of her head, holding her still while he brought his mouth down to hers. "Don't let it," he murmured against her lips and then pressed her back against the blanket, kissing her with a gentleness that had been missing the night before. Then there had been fierce need and hunger, passion that took her breath away and left her responding blindly and helplessly. But now his tongue was moving over hers with slow deliberation, his lips and teeth drawing her tongue into his mouth and urging her to explore him, too. His mouth still tasted like pears, and she gave herself over to learning the feel of the smooth, inner flesh of his lips, circling his tongue with her own and then pulling it into her mouth as though greedy for its nectar.

She was content to do nothing but kiss him, lying back on the blanket and holding his head in her hands, but his free hand began moving over the slippery fabric of her bathing suit, his palm lightly tantalizing the budding peaks of her nipples. He made no attempt to remove her suit or her shirt, but his fingers slid down the taut skin of her belly and unerringly centered on a point of increasing sensation at the apex of her thighs. Instinctively she started to push his hand away, feeling shy and too vulnerable, but he caught her hand and held it above her head so that she couldn't fight him. "Let me," he murmured against her ear. "There's nobody here, nobody can see." And then as though he didn't trust words alone to persuade her, his fingers trailed up the smooth flesh of her thigh, gently pushing it out, and leaving her open to his explorations.

Emma gasped at the renewed assault on her senses, feeling his stroking fingers through her suit as though she were naked. She clutched his head to the side of her face and tried to still the sudden thrust of her hips, but he whispered encouragement into her ear, and she was helpless against her own shattering climax.

Afterward she turned on her side and hid her face against him, feeling the need for shelter although she didn't know from what. She felt humbled but not humiliated, and sensed that he was making demands on her that she had never had to answer before. He had continued running his hand over her back and shoulders, but she could tell that he was no longer aroused. She closed her eyes and relaxed into the sensation of security, and gave a little jump of surprise when he spoke a few minutes later.

"You know, Em, there's no reason in the world why you couldn't finish college if you wanted to. You might have to commute down to the University of Connecticut, but you could arrange to have the time away from the station, couldn't you?"

His voice was considering as he absently continued stroking her, and she wondered how long he had been lying there planning her future for her. She jerked her head back in order to look at him, and saw the surprise in his eyes at her angry movement. "I could, could I? I don't remember asking for your opinion."

His hand stopped rubbing her back, and he raised up on one elbow and regarded her in confusion. "Sorry, I didn't mean to butt in."

Emma sat up and turned her back to him, staring blindly at the lake. "Yes, you did," she said in a nasty voice, and then some inner demon prompted her to go on despite every bit of wisdom she had. "It bothers you that I'm not very well educated, doesn't it?"

At that he sat up too, too close beside her when all she wanted from him now was distance. "I don't know what you're talking about. You know I don't care about that," he replied, the voice of reason.

"Yes, you do, or you wouldn't have brought it up," she persisted. "Tell me, have you been stewing over this all along, or did it just occur to you?"

"Dammit," he exclaimed, bringing his fist down on the grass beside him. "I said it doesn't bother me! It bothers you; that was one of the first things you said to me."

"I knew it would bother you. I was trying to warn you," she replied in a voice she didn't recognize, and then sat in stunned silence as she realized what she had just said. This wasn't like her, and she hadn't the faintest idea why she was behaving this way. She sat still for another

moment to wallow in the horrible sensation of arguing
with someone she knew was right, and then glanced cov-
ertly over at Simon. He was staring out at the water and
shaking his head in defeat, as though he were just now
realizing what kind of a shrew she was.

"I don't understand," he said. "You've brought it up
several times, as though the fact that you never finished
college made you inadequate or something, and I just
thought that if it bothered you, you should do something about it."

She sighed in resignation. "Yeah, okay," she said
weakly, barely audible. Her words had no effect. He was
still shaking his head and looking confused and a little
wary. She gathered her forces and made an enormous
effort. "You're right. I'm sorry."

After a moment he looked over at her, apparently beginning to see the humor in the situation. "I take it that's
kind of a sore subject, huh?"

She felt like squirming. "I guess I thought you were
trying to change me, and I don't like that."

"Why not?" She shrugged in answer, feeling childish
but unwilling to pursue it.

He continued to regard her, his eyes a paler blue than
usual, as though they had absorbed the color of the clear
spring sky above. "I think you're fine the way you are.
But you don't always seem to agree with me."

"I don't want to talk about it anymore," she said, too
hastily. He was pressing her to confront something unpleasant, and all she could do to protect herself was shut
him out.

After a moment's silence he abruptly got to his feet.
"Fine," he said, bending down to gather up the remains
of their picnic. "Ready to go home?"

Emma thought that the ride back was uncomfortably
silent, but by the time they reached her apartment, Si-

mon's customary good humor seemed to be restored. He was determined not to let any more squabbles mar the rest of the weekend, and Emma let herself be buoyed up by his mood until her enthusiasm was equal to his. They bought fresh trout for dinner and Simon sat in the kitchen while she fixed them, giving her a blow-by-blow account of his trip to Paris and keeping her so entertained that she was able to behead the fish without feeling her customary faintheartedness. He taught her his secret recipe for salad dressing, which he claimed was the only thing he knew how to cook, and seemed so proud of it that Emma almost refrained from showing him she had that very recipe in one of her cookbooks. She struggled with the temptation to bring him down a notch, and when he started teasing her about the last dinner they had eaten in her apartment, her baser instincts won and she gleefully disabused him of the notion that he had invented something special. They then took the rest of the wine and retired to the bubble bath, and Emma was persuaded, despite her own strict principles, to leave the dishes in the sink until morning.

By late Monday morning Simon started gathering his things back into his overnight bag. Emma had arranged for Nora to cover her spot at the station in the morning and intended to repay her by taking hers in the afternoon, and now she was trailing along behind Simon, picking up the tie he had forgotten and rescuing her toothpaste from his shaving kit. He was wearing jeans and his shirt was untucked, and while that made his legs look almost ridiculously long, she had to resist the temptation to creep up behind him and tuck it in so that she would have a better view of his narrow hips as he moved familiarly around her home. She was still in a state of astonishment that he seemed to like her as much as he did, even after she had been so horrible at the lake the day before. Love, she decided, was a humbling experience, and she was lost in contemplation of this fact when she realized she had been adroitly backed up against the bedroom wall. She tilted her head back and smiled.

"I'll see you next weekend?" he asked, bending down to nuzzle her cheek while his hands stroked the bare skin of her arms. She nodded, blissfully aware of how well her body fit into his. He raised his head to study her. "You think you could come in to New York Friday night or Saturday morning?"

Emma felt a hint of alarm. What she had been afraid of was already starting, and she wanted to resist it. "No," she balked, and then fell back on her old excuse. "I can't be away from the studio."

He looked skeptical. "You seem to have managed to be away from it this weekend."

"Well," she began, flustered. "It's true that I don't have to work but if anything should go wrong, I have to be here. It's part of owning your own business; it's worse than a baby," she finished, trying to laugh it off.

He started to reply, and then stopped himself. "At least babies can be potty trained," he commented lightly, bending down to kiss her goodbye. "I'll let you know when I'm coming."

She let him out and then went to the window to watch him walk to his car. She could tell he would grow dissatisfied with her soon. How could he not, when his life was so full, so fast-paced and exciting. She was half-tempted to end it now, to get the pain over with, because the longer she put it off, the worse it would be.

Moreover, the sooner it was over, the sooner she would be able to quiet her own self-doubts. He had roused certain possibilities she had not considered for a long time, and suddenly she no longer knew if she was genuinely satisfied with her life or if she accepted it because she was afraid she wasn't capable of any more. She was an expert on the big band era, had become one simply by listening, reading, talking to the people who knew it. But she had become an expert simply for the love of it, not for any publicity or even personal gain. And was that somehow cowardly? She used to have such a firm grip on her own standards and now it was slipping.

She didn't even know if she was honestly questioning her own values or if she was trying to be a woman who could hold on to a man like Simon Eliot. Not like him. *Him.* She thought she might still be something of a novelty for him, but if they were to have a future, she would have to enter his world, go back to New York and abandon everything that she had built over the years. And then she wouldn't be herself anymore, and not only would Simon probably stop liking her very much, she wouldn't care for herself much either. The pace of New York did not fit her. She practically underwent a chemical change after spending even a short time in the city, and her family had recognized it and stopped suggesting she come down. But Simon would not see it that way. She puttered about her apartment doing household chores, ran mindlessly through Nora's top-forty program in the afternoon, and finally went to bed early, depressed by a sense of futility.

Nine

———

"So when do we get to meet him?" Stu asked as Emma set a platter of steaming calzones on the table. It was a Wednesday night near the end of June and Marcy, at loose ends now that school was out, had come over to help her make the pockets of dough. They had gotten rather carried away when they started mixing up the savory cheese filling, adding prosciutto, bits of vegetables, and whatever else caught a ten-year-old's fancy until Emma had no idea just what it was that she was asking her friend to eat.

"I hope you like these," she replied lightly. "There are twelve of them and you're taking home whatever is left over. How about the Fourth of July weekend? He'll be here longer then. At least I guess he will—we haven't talked about it." Simon had been making the drive to Litchfield every weekend without complaint, sometimes arriving as late as Saturday afternoon and leaving twenty-four hours later, but never again had he suggested that she come to him for a change. They had had three wonderful weekends, weekends to be treasured, and Emma would have been happier than she had ever thought possible if she hadn't known that it couldn't last.

The problem was not with anything that Simon said or did. The problem was that she knew, in her heart, that he would not be satisfied with her forever, and that was exactly what she wanted. Hadn't he made subtle, or sometimes not so subtle, attempts to change her from the first moment they'd met? Teaching her to swim, encouraging her to go back to college and, more importantly, doing the presentation. He had not mentioned it once, but his very silence made it loom constantly in Emma's mind.

She knew he had not found anybody to do it yet, and she was waiting for him to approach her about it again, resenting him for not bringing it up and knowing she would resent him even more if he did. It wasn't as simple as doing a favor for him. What was unspoken and infuriating was Emma's conviction that Simon thought she *should* do it; and the fact that he had, in her mind anyway, already made a judgment prevented her from being able to figure out whether or not she thought she should do it.

It had grown from being a minor incident to being symbolic of Simon's feelings for her. He didn't, she decided, love her for what she was, and therein lay the root of the problem. For example, after she had refinished her pie safe, rubbed lavender oil into the shelves, stocked it with her linens and displayed it at the end of the hall, he had failed to comment on it. She had, finally, pointed it out to him.

"It looks terrific, sweetie," he had answered, but it was clear to her that he had been more interested at the time in holding her against him and nibbling at the side of her

neck. She realized he simply didn't care as much about it
as she did, but she had worked hard on it, and shouldn't
he have taken the time to examine it? This, too, became
symbolic.

And what was really intolerable was that she suspected she was being silly, that the things in her life that
were important to her weren't really important, that Simon's life was somehow more real. She kept this increasing paranoia bottled up inside herself, and the result
was that she was turning into a temperamental shrew.

She was lost in these discouraging reflections when she
felt a sharp jab on her shin and looked up with a start to
find Stu staring at her with a worried look on her face.
Her friend opened her mouth to say something but was
interrupted by a heartrending moan from the end of the
table.

"I'm so *bored*," Marcy said, putting her fork down in
despair. She had done nothing to her calzone but dissect
it, having more than satisfied her appetite during her ex-
ertions in the kitchen that afternoon, and was now looking at her mother and Emma accusingly. "I can't stand
being here anymore. Why does your friend keep coming
up? I mean, what do you guys find to do?"

Emma wanted to tell her, but Marcy's innocent words
provoked a sudden, unbidden image of herself and Simon, sitting side by side in her tub and letting their feet
dangle over the side, with very little concealed by mounds
of bubbles. She started to blush. "Well, I'm learning how
to swim. Do you ever go over to Bantam Lake or Waramaug?"

"All my friends are in camp," she replied, glaring at
her mother. "There's nobody here to go with me."

"You said you didn't want to go to camp this year,
honey pot," Stu answered, clearly not seeing her daughter's problem for the tragedy it was.

"Well, you should have known I'd be bored. You should have made me go!"

"Marcy, you were adamant," she replied. "That means that you wouldn't let me change your mind. If you'll remember, I did try. Now I'm sorry you're bored, but I refuse to take the blame. If there's anything I can do to entertain you, I'll be happy to, but you'll have to think of it yourself."

Emma had watched the little drama with a gleam of amusement in her eye. When the ten-year-old was suitably quelled and humbled, she broke in. "I'll tell you what, Marcy. If the weather is nice this weekend and Simon and I decide to go to the lake, do you want to come swimming? He might even take you out on a sailboat, but I can't promise."

Marcy considered it for a moment, knowing the importance of not appearing too eager. "Yes, I'd like that."

"Okay," Emma said. "If it's not raining." The rest of the dinner was spent in a long, friendly gossip between the two women while Marcy, to her credit, cleaned up the kitchen and looked through Emma's collection of music boxes. By the time Emma was ready for bed, she realized she hadn't worried about the basic worth of her life for several hours, and was grateful to Marcy for her timely interruption.

As luck would have it, two nights later when Simon finally stood up from his desk and walked over to the wide picture window in his office overlooking the park, it was to admire the thunderstorm that was just beginning to rumble out in the distance. Simon loved a good storm, and his only wish was that Emma were there and he could wrap his arms around her, rest his chin on her head, and watch it with her. He was imagining that she was with him more and more lately, using her presence as a bribe to help get through the week. He was in a fair way to becoming obsessed with her, and that fact was worrying him more than a little.

Simon had known several weeks before that he was falling for her harder than he'd ever fallen for anyone, but he had handled it by resolutely declining to worry about the future. He hadn't allowed himself to worry, throwing himself into his work during the week with more than his customary gusto and then giving himself over to the joy of her company on weekends. Because of the size of his workload, he had to work overtime just to have those weekends and was, for the first time, wishing he had more time to spend away from work. The fact that Simon Eliot kept coming back to, the fact that made him look up from his desk and let his stare rest blindly on the vista before him in blank puzzlement, was that his full life had heretofore been seriously lacking in something. For the first time he was beginning to suspect that his constant activity served to conceal from himself that he was lonely.

Lonely. Simon pondered the word as he tossed his overnight bag into the car the next morning for the drive to Litchfield. He was later than usual because he had forced himself not to hurry, forced himself to try to think calmly about what was happening. For one thing, he knew it was absurd to drive up for a weekend in the country when the rain was still drumming steadily on the roof of his car. If they could only spend the weekend in New York, the rain wouldn't interfere. He would, he thought, like to take Emma to the opera and then to a late dinner in one of the thousands of tiny, excellent little restaurants in mid-Manhattan. He wondered if she liked Japanese food and if she'd let him take her to his favorite restaurant and order for her. He wanted to show her things. He was suddenly seeing New York as a city for lovers, and he wanted his to be there.

On the other hand, he knew he appreciated the city more lately because he spent so little time there. He had realized with a shock that there was, in fact, another way to live, a way he had forgotten about because he had put up with city life, high-rise life, for so long. But there were things that shouldn't have to be merely put up with, but enjoyed.

Rain, for example. It was true there were many things to do to amuse oneself in New York when it was rainy, but they were each based on the premise that it was desirable to avoid getting wet. A summer rainstorm in Litchfield, Connecticut, seemed by contrast full of possibilities. One wouldn't object to having that rain on one's person. He could imagine opening the windows simply to smell the air, with no risk of being joined by a filthy pigeon looking for shelter.

He amused himself with further comparisons, but he knew it wasn't the Litchfield/New York relationship that was bothering him as much as the Emma/Simon relationship. It was not always easy to make the trip to the country on the weekend, but what bothered him was that he was always going to *her* place. He wanted equal footing in the relationship. He wanted to be more than a weekend lover, and he suspected that Emma's life simply did not have room for him. He was too big and clumsy. He broke her little wineglasses and his feet dangled over the foot of the bed. The outward signs told him plainly that he did not fit, and he was not sure what the solution was.

He thought back to the beginning of their relationship, when he had first realized he envied her. She had been completely out of step with the rest of his life, their weekends a series of snatched interludes in which nothing seemed to matter except the two of them. The problem was that he wanted, needed, more of her and he wanted her to want it too. It wasn't enough that she continued to let him come up. He wanted her to commit herself to the relationship as he felt he had, and he wasn't even sure how he wanted her to do it.

He found a place to park in front of the house she lived in and contemplated the rain running in wide rivers down his windshield. He was beginning to think, with genuine shock, that he wanted to get married, but he was the consummate bachelor, and it simply wasn't a part of his plans to tie himself down to one woman, no matter how irresistible she was, no matter how she dogged his thoughts whenever he was away from her, no matter that he was acting like an idiot driving up to see her at every opportunity. But he was, and there was nothing he could do about it. After years of a carefree existence, Simon had stumbled across someone he didn't want to live without. And it was really infuriating, now that he was suffering so, that Emma seemed to be able to live without him just fine. He didn't think it would be wise to reveal this newly discovered vulnerability just yet, but it was becoming intolerable to keep it to himself, and the whole mess was making him irritable. He grabbed his bag and ran up the path to the front door, determined to handle this problem in his usual style and simply not think about it for a while.

When Emma opened the door to him, smiling her customary warm smile, his first impulse was to rage and throw his large frame around her tiny apartment. She had apparently been spending the morning in household chores. The little room was tidy and fairly glistened, and her checkbook and canceled checks were spread across the coffee table. Emma had been going over her accounts, keeping her life in order, calmly managing day-to-day existence, and Simon couldn't stand it. He managed to greet her with a fair amount of civility, and submitted to having his hair dried off with a towel. When she sat down on his lap and seemed inclined to stay there, however, his patience began to wear thin.

"No swimming lesson today, huh?" she asked. He grunted in reply. "That's too bad," she went on, undaunted. "I was going to race you to the float."

"What do you have planned instead?" he asked in a surly voice.

She looked at him in surprise. "Well, I guess I haven't given it much thought."

"Too bad we're not in New York. Plenty of things to do there."

Emma knew his words were justified to some extent, but he hadn't made any mention of meeting in the city, and she had supposed he liked getting away from it on weekends. "Well, we're not," she began reasonably and then added, "I thought you liked coming up here."

He gave an unkind snort. "In weather like this?"

"Well, Simon, I apologize for the weather but there's nothing I can do about it," she said in a huffy voice, struggling to get off his lap and finding it impossible. Simon's fingers had slipped into her waistband and held her firmly in place. She turned around to glare at him.

"I'm sorry," he said mildly. "If I promise to behave, will you stay on my lap?" She nodded, eyeing him mistrustfully. He held her closer, burying his face in her hair. "I love coming up here, but sometimes it's hard to find the time. I need for you to meet me halfway." She didn't respond, and when he held her away to look into her face, her eyes were wide and dry and it was impossible for him to tell what she was thinking. He decided to be a coward and not try to find out.

Eight hours later it was still raining. Emma loved lying in bed listening to the patter on the roof and watching the drops, highlighted by a distant streetlamp, course down the windowpane. She felt at peace and content, but she sensed a restlessness in Simon, felt that something was building inside him. They had had a quiet afternoon and then had driven over to have dinner at one of the inns on Waramaug, what they had come to consider "their" lake. They ate a leisurely meal and then sat out on the covered veranda and gazed out over the water in the dark. They hadn't spoken much, had talked only of inconsequential matters, but she could tell there was some topic they were avoiding, and she didn't know what to do about it. It was out of character for Simon to brood, but his blue eyes were as dark and overcast as the sky, and his mood was unusually quiet.

She was afraid to ask what he had meant earlier when he said he needed her to meet him halfway. She had no strenuous objection to going to New York for an occasional weekend, but hot summer weekends in the city were something she had always detested. No, what he was really asking her to do was change, learn to fit into his life or lose him.

He was waiting, she was convinced, for her to agree to make the speech for him at the dinner. By virtue of the fact that she thought about doing it four or five times a day, she was now convinced that she couldn't. It had grown from a simple introduction of a man whose work she knew well to a project of monumental proportions. Emma now saw a crowd of thousands just waiting for her to make a fool of herself. Her various and valid reasons for saying no in the first place had become overshadowed by a single prevailing one—fear. And every time she realized that, she remembered Simon's telling her months ago that fear wasn't a good reason not to do something. He simply asked too much of her, and she was afraid he was getting ready to again.

Even the way they had made love had been different. He had seemed almost hesitant, even sorrowful, at first, touching her with uncharacteristic gentleness and then forcing her to take a more active role than usual, pulling her on top of him and guiding her hands and her mouth. Emma always loved to please him, but usually the first time they made love after a week apart he seemed too starved for her to tolerate for long her more teasing, tender touch. He whipped them both into a frenzy and then later would let her have her way. And now he was lying quietly beneath her, rhythmically stroking her back while she rested her cheek on his burly chest and waited helplessly for him to start talking.

Without warning, his arms tightened around her and he rolled over and trapped her underneath him. "Emma, do you love me?" he asked, surprising her even further.

"Yes," she said, her voice turning to a whisper as she looked into his searching eyes. "Can't you tell?"

"No. No, I can't. I need for you to show me," he answered, his hand coming down to clamp the top of her head and imprison her gaze as effectively as he imprisoned her body. It was a little like being questioned by a well-meaning grizzly bear, and Emma knew there was no escape. "When are you going to start opening up to me, hmh? You haven't made any demands on me since I got back from France. Are you afraid to?" She made no answer, but she closed her eyes and her heart started thumping heavily. "There is something coming between us and I'm not going to let up on you until you start helping me figure out what it is. I'm not a patient man, and this matters too much for me to be able to sit around and wait until you decide to trust me."

"I do trust you," she said, opening her eyes and looking up into his intent face. It was the truth, because she knew he would never be intentionally cruel. He could hurt her so easily, but she knew that when he did, it would be because of the way they both were, because their lives could never meet. She understood that, but she knew he would never accept that she couldn't change for him.

"But what is it that you want?" he persisted. "Sometimes I think you expect this to be just a temporary affair, and in a little while we'll both go our separate ways. But that's not what *I* want," he said, giving her a little shake. "I'm tired of not having you be a part of the rest of my life, my real life." He rolled off her to lie on his back and contemplate the ceiling.

Several long minutes ticked by, while Emma lay beside him feeling paralyzed. She was being rushed, she thought. Maybe she could do what he wanted if he gave her time, but he was rushing her. As though he were reading her mind, Simon turned toward her and propped his head up on his arm. "Listen to me, Em. I'm not sure how much you wanted to get involved with me in the first place. Maybe I pushed you into it, and maybe for some reason you let me. But I can't keep being the only one whose doing any pushing."

Something in the finality of his tone penetrated Emma's sense of panic. With startling clarity she realized that if she didn't do something, she was going to lose him. She had been dreading this moment forever and now that it was here, she couldn't stand it. "What do you want me to do?" she asked woodenly.

Simon sighed in frustration. "I guess it's not really that simple. It's supposed to come from you, and maybe there's nothing there. You tell me."

"I don't know why we can't just go on as we have been," she finally answered, gripped by panic and feeling it was useless anyway. The subject had been brought up and it wouldn't just go away. She supposed neither one of them had taken love seriously enough, trying to behave as though it wouldn't necessarily change their lives, and now they were paying the penalty. If it was only her life that had to change, she could accept it. But Simon was asking her to change herself. Suddenly she was angry. "Listen, Simon, this is what I am. It's the best I can do, and I've been doing just fine for thirty years. You'll have to just take me or...or leave me."

She didn't look at him, watching instead as the rain drummed heavily against the window. After a long silence, he finally said lightly, "I've already taken you. I'm not sure I can manage again just yet."

"It's not funny," she answered with a quaver in her voice. "If you don't want me for what I am, you can just put on your clothes and leave."

This time she looked over at him and saw a gleam of amusement in his eyes. "You would kick me out at one o'clock in the morning in the rain? Where's your sense of compassion?"

"Simon!" she exclaimed, sitting up and turning around to glare down at him. At that he laughed out loud and, to her fury, grabbed her arms and pulled her down to lie against his chest. "Stop being such a bully, Simon," she said, her voice dripping with contempt. "You think you can have your way because you're big enough to push me around."

"So fight back."

"I'll hurt you," she replied, her eyes narrowing.

"Be my guest."

He had a tight grip on her wrists. Emma stared down at him while her mother's voice echoed in her memory—

If a man tries to take advantage of you, knee him in the groin. She mustered every bit of decency she had left, closed her mind to maternal maxims, and sank her teeth viciously in his belly.

He groaned. "Would you do that again, a little lower?" When she jerked her head up in dismay he chuckled and pulled her up to lie on her side facing him. He cuddled her close, absently patting her fanny as though he were trying to soothe her. "Let's not worry about it for now," he said, his voice close to her ear. He was holding her against him, resting his head on top of hers, engulfing her in his large, hairy body. Emma mumbled an affirmative, unable to do more with her face squashed between his head and the pillow, and eventually they went to sleep.

Emma was grateful to see the sun shining when she woke up, and even more grateful when she remembered her promise to Marcy to take her to the lake. Simon agreed docilely enough, only remarking when they were on the way to pick her up that he didn't know any ten-year-olds. Emma had not even thought about whether or not they would get along, and she found herself being amused at the way they silently sized each other up as soon as the little girl climbed into the back seat of the car. "Marcy, this is Simon. Simon, Marcy," she said casually.

"Hi, Marcy," he said, not offering to shake hands, or be too friendly, or do anything that might make her uncomfortable.

"Hi," she answered shyly. She said nothing else until they were almost at the lake, and Simon let himself be studied in silence. When they reached the road that circled its border, she finally spoke. "Are we going to rent a sailboat?"

"Do you know how to sail?" he asked.

"No."

"Willing to learn?"

"Yes."

"Sure, we can rent a sailboat. We'll have to wear life jackets, though. I can't afford to lose a member of the crew." At that he glanced over at Emma and saw that she was leaning against the door with a secret little grin on her face. She had managed to avoid the life-jacket problem by insisting that now she knew how to swim, so there was no need.

"Well, I'm going to swim out to the float and fall asleep, so you guys keep it down out there."

"You won't go with us?" Marcy asked instantly.

Emma turned and looked into the back seat. "There's only room for two," she said with a reassuring smile. Marcy looked at Simon's dark head, looked back at Emma, stared out the window in indecision, and then apparently decided not to pass up a good opportunity.

"Okay," she said serenely.

After that one brief hesitation, the morning ran perfectly smoothly. Marcy had, with apparently pure animal instinct, decided Simon was acceptable and threw herself wholeheartedly into her sailing lesson. Emma could hear her laughing and chattering from halfway across the lake and Simon, for reasons of his own, seemed to be enjoying himself almost as much. She smiled and stretched lazily against the weathered planks of the float in the lake, and only woke up when she was joined by two dripping wet and overly enthusiastic bodies.

Emma was a little apprehensive after they had deposited a slightly sunburnt Marcy back on her doorstep and headed for home. Although Simon had not indicated any desire to continue their discussion of the night before, she could never tell when he was going to bring up something that she would rather not talk about. He acted as though he had forgotten all about it until he had showered and tossed his clothes back into his overnight bag. He stood by the door, looking down at her, and Emma felt more than her customary sense of desolation at the thought that he was leaving for another week.

"Emma," he said gently, cupping her face in his hands and stroking her cheek with one thumb. "Nobody's going to make you do something you don't want to do."

"I know," she said in a choked whisper.

"Kiss me goodbye," he said, and she stood on tiptoe and wrapped both arms tightly around him, burying her face in his neck, overwhelmed suddenly by a sense of desolation and bereavement. He let her cling to him for several seconds and then pulled her head back and started kissing her mouth with a feeling of desperation he had been able to keep in check until then. She was responding to him fully, but just as she tried to pull his body in closer to hers, he stepped away from her abruptly, and after one more look, he was out the door and down the stairs.

Emma stared at the wooden panel before her in stunned silence. How had this mess happened, she wondered. But she knew exactly what had happened. Her little magic kingdom had been invaded. She was too confused at the moment to decide if she was lucky or unlucky, but she knew for a certainty that the only thing to do now was curl up on the couch with the faithful Percy and subject herself to a painful and unrelenting scrutiny.

Ten

By Monday morning Emma had come to several unappealing conclusions. One of them was that Simon was absolutely right, that she had been letting him make most of the effort in the relationship because she was afraid of being hurt once she committed herself. Another was that they couldn't simply keep going on as they had before. It wasn't honest, it wouldn't work and it wasn't what she wanted. And the final conclusion was that she didn't know what to do about any of it.

What she wanted to do was call Simon, or better yet, go see him and say, "Please help me." She didn't know how to do what he wanted her to do, and she wanted more than anything to learn. He seemed so much better at love than she was. But that wasn't fair to him, either, and it was time she started being fair. She had to do something to prove herself; she had to, as it were, put up some collateral, say "This is what it is worth to me to have another chance.'' Because it was clear from the weekend that she had about run out of chances. She had been holding back, and now she was all too likely to end up with nothing.

A sultry haze of heat had descended over town, and by the time she got to the studio to do some paperwork she was soaked with perspiration, and her mood had grown, if anything, worse. Apparently she wasn't the only one to be feeling it. Nora had just finished running through the news and local announcements and gave her the limpest of greetings before turning back to the console.

As she was sitting in her office a few minutes later her employee appeared in the doorway with a sheaf of papers in her hand. ''Emma, when are you going to get around to looking at your mail?''

''Is there anything important?'' she asked, glancing up from a bank statement.

''It's mostly junk. Two bills came yesterday, but this letter has been sitting out there for two weeks,'' Nora said, depositing the pile on her desk with a rather dusty-looking envelope on top.

''Why am I just getting it now?'' she asked, irritated.

''Why do you never look in your In box?'' the younger woman snapped.

''Touché,'' Emma muttered. She tore open the envelope and glanced down at the signature. Marion Black, assistant to Jack Morissey. The name rang a bell, but she couldn't quite remember where she had heard it.

By the time she had digested the contents of the letter, she remembered all too well. Jack Morissey was directing the documentary on Willis Edmonds that was to use a testimonial dinner in his honor as a starting point. Mr. Edmonds was going to be ninety years old on Thursday, and they were looking for someone knowledgeable about the big band era to introduce him, since so many people didn't really remember who he was. Ms. Black had come across some articles Emma had written and wondered if she might be of any help, if she could suggest someone for the job, or even better, give a short speech herself. She would be most appreciative of anything Emma could do on such short notice, and she hoped to hear from her soon. Sincerely.

Emma put the letter down with a queer feeling in her stomach. There was no mention of Simon, but there had to be a connection. Was this what he had been referring to last weekend, her silence in response to a direct and very professional appeal? And why pretend they had only found her through a series of articles she had written a year and a half ago?

She reached for the telephone without hesitation. She was appalled that Marion Black had been waiting all this time to hear from her, and she wanted to remedy that right away. She had already given her name to the receptionist and was waiting for Ms. Black to pick up the phone when she realized she still wasn't quite sure what her answer was going to be.

When the conversation was over, Emma put down the phone and turned to stare out the window with a glazed look on her face. It had all been effortless, and she realized to her very real shame that if she had been approached that way in the first place, she would have agreed to do the presentation almost without hesitation. She would have been nervous, certainly, but she would have been flattered to have been asked. Instead, she had been suspicious of Simon's motives, suspicious even of her own brother.

Emma finally realized that for all her solitude and supposed introspection, she did not really know herself. She had been so defensive of her own lifestyle only because she was not convinced it was right for her, and not because anyone else seriously threatened it. When people remarked, as they usually did at some point, that it was unusual for her to live the way she did coming from the family she came from, she was able to convince them it was what she genuinely wanted, but she had not, up to this point, been able to convince herself. She was guilty of trying to live by someone else's standards, and what she finally saw now was that when a person reached the age of thirty, no one expected her to live by standards other than her own. What it came down to now was simply that she had underestimated everyone she was close to. It wasn't that they didn't care how she lived—it was that they genuinely loved her for what she was.

Now, according to the agreement she had reached with Marion Black, she would go to New York and give her speech and satisfy herself that she could do it. She would go with an open mind, and then honestly decide how she felt about it, rather than trying to determine how other people felt she ought to feel. If they cared about her, they wanted her to be happy in any way she could, and if they didn't care about her, their opinions were inconsequential. It was surprisingly logical once she stopped being so paranoid.

The last of the paranoia had surfaced and been dismissed in the brief conversation with Ms. Black. After she had apologized profusely for ignoring the letter and confirmed that they still had no one to speak, and that Marion was afraid she would have to give a short and unsatisfactory introduction herself, she asked, "Didn't you get my name from Simon Eliot?"

"Oh no, Mr. Eliot's just the producer," she was told. "He doesn't concern himself with details like this. Now, he did say he had a lead on a couple of possibilities last spring, but then he said they both fell through, and he dumped the whole thing in my lap."

"I see," Emma had responded, seeing clearly for the first time, and had gone on to discuss such important matters as what she should wear and when she should be there. Simon had told her long before that he accepted her refusal at face value and she had always known, if she bothered to pay attention to what she knew, that he meant what he said. It was an admirable quality and one that she hoped she would learn to adopt herself. She was an immature, paranoid, deluded fool, she told herself as she stood and hastily bunched the half-finished financial statements into an untidy pile. She went out in search of something to wear that would, perhaps, help her convince Simon to ignore the fact that she was such a horrible person.

By early afternoon on Thursday she was on her way. She had made elaborate preparations for the trip, buying two dresses because she could not decide which was more appropriate, going to the beauty shop for a much needed trim, leaving the car at the gas station to have the oil changed, the brakes tested and the tires rotated. She had arranged for Marcy to stop in and feed Percy, play with him and give him the emotional support she thought he needed to survive her absence—Percy pretended not to love her but she could see through him.

She considered letting Simon know she was coming, but decided against it. For one thing, it would have more impact if she actually showed up, in the flesh, and did the speech than if she prepared him for the surprise. She was also half hoping that he wouldn't be at the dinner, although she knew the chances of that were slim. She would be a lot less nervous if he weren't there, because despite the fact that her project for the week had been to get ready for the dinner, she had done everything except prepare what she was going to say.

Emma knew that wasn't particularly smart and the only reason she did it was that she had absolutely no idea what she *should* say. She kept postponing that little project, hoping to have time to give it some serious thought on the drive down. Perhaps it was because her mind was so preoccupied that she managed to turn the wrong way after she had crossed the Triboro bridge.

Perhaps, she thought as she gritted her teeth and tried to ignore the obscenities of the man whose legs she had nearly amputated when he stepped in front of her car. Or perhaps it was like a Freudian slip, her subconscious preventing her from doing something she wasn't entirely sure she wanted to do. She had hit a bad bit of preweekend traffic, and now a couple of traffic jams were all it would take to make her late for the dinner. Her situation was complicated, moreover, by the fact that she was seriously lost. The traffic was moving ahead with mindless determination and Emma moved along with it, unable to see any place to pull over that wasn't already filled with double-parked cars. She had managed to glimpse a street sign, however, and knew that she was on Adam Clayton Powell Jr. Boulevard.

Emma had never heard of Adam Clayton Powell Jr. Boulevard. Put her on Park Avenue and she could orient herself in a jiffy, but the only thing she knew now was that she was still on the island of Manhattan. She was beginning to suspect with a fair amount of certainty that she was on very much the wrong end of the island, and she hunched forward over her steering wheel to see what she could deduce from the occasional visible names of the side streets she was passing.

The first numbered street did not make her feel very confident. It was One hundred and thirty-fifth Street, and Emma had never been above Eighty-sixth Street in her life. Her old neighborhood was about one hundred

and fifty blocks south and she wondered just how far up
the island went. Trying hard to be an optimist, she told
herself it was possible she was heading in the right direction, and she searched for another street that actually had
its sign intact and facing the street. One hundred and
forty-second Street. Wrong way. Her mouth was dry with
panic, and two more blocks went by before she realized
that she simply had to turn off this street and go back the
other way. She was vainly hoping for the chance to make
a right turn when she saw a large bridge looming directly
in front of her, spanning what she knew must be the East
River, and beyond that a sign directing her to Yankee
Stadium.

Without giving the matter any rational thought at all,
she brought her foot down on the gas, wrenched the car
around to the left, and turned in front of several lanes of
oncoming traffic, narrowly missing the front end of a bus
and the tail of a long and rather rusty pink Cadillac. The
bus driver's horror stricken face as he stepped on the
brake was imprinted in her mind's eye, and she drove into
a gloomy and narrow side street and pulled over immediately, clenching her hands between her knees until she
had stopped shaking. All she knew was that Yankee
Stadium was in the Bronx and that once she left Manhattan she would never again find her way back in. She
had been right in the first place, she should never have
stirred from her cozy little apartment and the next time
someone tried to prod her into doing something she was
not inclined to do, she was going to...

Emma took a deep breath and steadied herself as her
common sense gradually became restored to her. This
little trip was her idea, it was still a good idea, and she
was perfectly capable of finding her way to the hotel in
plenty of time for the speech. She hadn't been in New
York for some time, but there was bound to be a logical

solution to her dilemma. She could, of course, find a phone booth and call Marion Black, but not only would that make her feel silly, it would also necessitate getting out of the car and she wasn't convinced that would be wise. She looked around, seeing that she was on a quiet street with trees along one side, casting definitely lengthening shadows.

It seemed to be an innocuous, peaceful little residential street, its brownstone houses tidy although they had clearly seen many better days. But to Emma it looked like the kind of street where one would hide the bodies of one's recently murdered victims and she had to stop herself from stomping on the gas pedal and speeding away in another fit of panic. She glanced around to assure herself that her doors were locked, and thought carefully about what she should do.

She knew she wanted to go to the left. She knew there were only a few broad avenues running the length of Manhattan. Therefore the logical move was to drive straight ahead until she found a likely looking street going in the right direction. Encouraged, she moved ahead cautiously and was rewarded several blocks later with the discovery of Broadway. Broadway, she knew, would take her where she wanted to go. Twenty minutes later, weak but triumphant, she was searching for a parking place within a couple of blocks of the hotel.

Emma was never able to remember later exactly what it was she finally said to introduce Willis Edmonds. When she walked into the hotel, Marion Black was pacing the floor, watching for her with a frantic look on her face and asking passing strangers if they happened to be Emma Beckett. Seeing the other woman's panic, Emma was suddenly calm.

"Ms. Black, I'm so sorry to have kept you waiting. I lost my way and then had to fight the traffic to get here."

"Oh, Ms. Beckett, there you are," she said, gripping Emma's hands in her sweaty palms and pulling her into the elevator. "I'm so worried the whole thing is going to flop."

Ms. Black looked to be all of twenty-three, and Emma felt sorry for her. "How is it going so far?" she asked.

"It's going fine, but you know *anything* could happen. And Mr. Eliot is sitting right out there and I didn't even think he was going to come," she ended with a slight wail.

Emma's heart started to thud uncomfortably. "I know him," she mentioned casually. "Do you suppose he knows I'm speaking?"

"Well, of course you're listed on the program," Marion answered. "You'll have a chance to talk to him, though. I put you at his table, and after you freshen up we can go right in. I'm afraid you've only got twenty minutes to eat your dinner but I had them keep it hot."

Emma's stomach was now filled with a hoard of very angry butterflies. "Oh, I never eat before I speak," she said with entirely false assurance. "And I'll see Simon after the program. If it's all right with you, I'll just look over my notes before I have to go on."

That was fine with Marion Black and if Emma only had some notes to look over, she would have been quite content. She sat just off the stage, where she could see Marion well enough to receive her signal but couldn't see anybody else. All too soon, however, she saw the young woman catch her eye and nod, and she took a deep breath and walked onto the stage.

She didn't need to look around to see Simon. She could feel him, sitting at a table in the front and to her left, and she was careful not to look at him because she had no idea what would happen when she did. "Hello, music lovers, and jazz lovers, and lovers of Willis Edmonds," she began, looking instead at an old and very tiny man sitting almost directly in front of her, and smiled her warmest smile. Willis Edmonds smiled back, and Emma suddenly found it very easy to tell the audience just who he was, what he had done, and why they should all be grateful for his presence among them. She spoke for about fifteen minutes, and when the guest of honor rose at the end and made his way slowly to the microphone, she joined the applause, stepped back off the stage, and resumed her seat in the wings.

When it was over, she walked out and found Simon standing by his table, arms folded across his chest, paying no attention to the crowd milling around him. She stepped up to him and shyly touched his elbow, and when he looked down at her she saw he wore a puzzled, guarded expression. "Do you have time to take a walk with me?" he asked after studying her for a couple of minutes.

"Sure," she answered, following him out a side door and walking along beside him in silence. The murky heat wave that had gripped Litchfield was magnified several times by the buildings and pavement as well as by the lack of cool greenery, and the silk of Emma's dress formed a sticky, second skin before they had gone two blocks. Simon kept striding ahead as though he had a pressing engagement, however, and she kept up with him without complaining. "Uh, how did I do?" she asked after ten minutes had gone by.

"Fine."

Emma doubted the sincerity of his answer. "Would you happen to remember what I said? Because I have no idea," she said, in an attempt to be lighthearted. She had not really planned this part of the evening, either, and was having considerably more trouble ad-libbing.

"I really wasn't paying attention, Emma," he confessed offhandedly and then looked at her in surprise when she stopped short.

"Well, for Pete's sake—" she began.

"Emma!" he interrupted her sharply and then, taking her arm, added gently, "You're ruining your shoes."

She looked down dumbly and saw that yes, indeed, she was ruining them, standing midstream in the outflow of an open fire hydrant a half block away. It was a common enough sight in the summer, a group of children playing in the gushing stream from an open hydrant, but Emma gazed vacantly at the scene without hearing the shrieks and giggles. She let Simon help her onto a dry patch of concrete but refused to budge after that. "Where are we going?"

"To my apartment," he said, tightening his grip on her arm preparatory to taking her there by force if need be.

"Not until you tell me why you didn't listen," she insisted, trying to pull her arm free and maintain her dignity at the same time.

"Because I was too busy trying to figure out why you didn't tell me you were going to speak!" he said, gripping her other arm and half lifting her off her feet so that she could look directly into his face and therefore not mistake the full force of his anger.

Emma wished she had a good answer to that. "I guess I thought I'd surprise you," she said weakly, vaguely aware that the noise up the block had quieted somewhat.

"Hmmm," Simon responded, signifying disapproval.

"And I also wanted to prove I could do it," she added quickly.

"Prove it to me?" he asked in surprise, too surprised to remember to let go of her arms now that his anger was fading. "I never doubted you could do it."

"Maybe to prove it to both of us," she confessed. "Listen, Simon, I want to be with you more than anything, but I am what I am and I just can't be *me* in New York. I don't want to be a part of it. I love my life in Connecticut, and my radio station, and...and my pie safe and all those things that you may think are stupid, but that's what I am. I don't know exactly what it is you want me to do, but I just can't do it in this city."

Simon started to smile but stopped himself. "I just want to be a part of your life, Em. That's why I was angry that you hadn't told me you were coming, because I thought you were still shutting me out. I know you don't want to come back to New York, and I wouldn't change a thing about you. I happened to have grown very fond of Litchfield, you know. Don't you know I love everything about you?"

"You do?"

He nodded firmly. "Emma, would you and your pie safe marry me?"

At that Emma gave in to her natural inclination and pulled his face down to hers, oblivious of the whistles and rude gestures of their adolescent audience up the block. "I love you, Simon," she whispered against his mouth.

After several long minutes, Simon pulled away and nuzzled his lips next to her ear. "Em, don't you think you could do it in the city just this once?"

The Silhouette Cameo Tote Bag Now available for just $6.99

Handsomely designed in blue and bright pink, its stylish good looks make the Cameo Tote Bag an attractive accessory. The Cameo Tote Bag is big and roomy (13″ square), with reinforced handles and a snap-shut top. You can buy the Cameo Tote Bag for $6.99, plus $1.50 for postage and handling.

Send your name and address with check or money order for $6.99 (plus $1.50 postage and handling), a total of $8.49 to:

Silhouette Books
120 Brighton Road
P.O. Box 5084
Clifton, NJ 07015-5084
ATTN: Tote Bag

SIL-T-1R

The Silhouette Cameo Tote Bag can be purchased pre-paid only. No charges will be accepted. Please allow 4 to 6 weeks for delivery.

N.Y. State Residents Please Add Sales Tax

Offer not available in Canada.

READERS' COMMENTS ON · SILHOUETTE DESIRES

"Thank you for Silhouette Desires. They are the best thing that has happened to the bookshelves in a long time."

—V.W.*, Knoxville, TN

"Silhouette Desires—wonderful, fantastic—the best romance around."

—H.T.*, Margate, N.J.

"As a writer as well as a reader of romantic fiction, I found DESIREs most refreshingly realistic—and definitely as magical as the love captured on their pages."

—C.M.*, Silver Lake, N.Y.

"I just wanted to let you know how very much I enjoy your Silhouette Desire books. I read other romances, and I must say your books rate up at the top of the list."

—C.N.*, Anaheim, CA

"Desires are number one. I especially enjoy the endings because they just don't leave you with a kiss or embrace; they finish the story. Thank you for giving me such reading pleasure."

—M.S.*, Sandford, FL

*names available on request

Silhouette Books

brings you the best in contemporary romance.

SILHOUETTE ROMANCE—contemporary romances that depict all the wonder and magic of falling in love.

SILHOUETTE DESIRE—more sensual, provocative stories of modern women in realistic situations.

SILHOUETTE SPECIAL EDITION—longer contemporary romances, emphasizing emotion as well as heightened romantic tension. And SILHOUETTE SPECIAL EDITIONs are sensuous and believable love stories.

AND NOW

SILHOUETTE INTIMATE MOMENTS—love stories with the one element no one else has tapped: excitement. They are longer, more sensuous romance novels filled with adventure, suspense, glamour or melodrama.